POOR MISS COLE AND THE COBBLER'S BOY

VICTORIAN ROMANCE

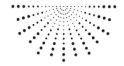

ROSIE SWAN

PUREREAD.COM

CONTENTS

CHAPTER ONE

Bristol, Southwest England, 1865

A mountain of white sails billowed on the horizon as the tea clipper raced towards the docks. A man stood at the pointed prow of the ship, pointing at the crowd waiting for them on land and shouting to the rest of the men, who expertly shifted the sails to make their approach.

Cecil Fontaine sat atop the railing, clinging for dear life with his small hands on either side. The crowd jostled around him, risking knocking him straight down into the water, but Cecil was too short to see otherwise, and he had not been here since dawn to miss the grand arrival.

The ship was called *The Taeping*, and Cecil had watched it leave the docks about seven months before. People said it was the fastest ship to have ever been built, although no one had officially tested that theory. It had travelled all the way to the other side of the world to China to load up with tea and then carry it all the way across the ocean back to England, and Cecil had been following news of the ship as closely as he could. It had left the East in late May, and it was only early September now, and yet, somehow, it had already circumnavigated the globe and arrived back home.

Watching the arrival of the great ships was something of a pastime in Bristol, and Cecil tried to never miss an important ship. If he had to miss school or face his mother's wrath, then so be it, as long as he was here to see the grandest ships come in from all around the globe. He had seen ships that had been to the Americas, to India, even to Australia, carrying riches to fill English food cupboards and shop shelves. Tea, spices, coffee, all cotton all travelled across the sea to reach Bristol, and it thrilled Cecil to imagine the adventures that the boats carrying them must have had on the way.

The crowd cheered and waved as *The Taeping* began to dock, and Cecil jumped down from the railing and pushed his way around people's legs to get closer to the point where the sailors themselves would disembark. At nine years' old, he was still small and skinny enough to navigate a crowd without anyone really noticing he was there, and he burst through just as the captain was making his way off the ship onto the dock.

"Sir!" Cecil shouted. "Sir! How much tea did you bring back, sir?"

Several other people were shouting at the captain, and he did not seem to hear Cecil's cries. The captain had dark, sun-damaged skin and a bushy grey beard, and he lurched unsteadily as he stepped onto land, as the sailors often did after a long voyage. But Cecil would not be discouraged by the captain's apparent disinterest.

"Sir!" he said again. "Sir, did you see any whales? Did you see sharks? Were there pirates, sir?"

The captain was not listening, and the other men did not seem to hear him either. They were too busy clapping one another on the back, congratulating themselves. Cecil scurried after the captain again, and he watched as the old man considered a large crate, nodded to himself in satisfaction, and then leapt atop it.

"Ladies and gentlemen!" the captain shouted to the crowd, and the crowd hushed. "Thank you all for greeting us today. It's so good to see other human faces after three months at sea. Especially some pretty ladies." He winked at one young woman, who blushed and giggled. "But now we've got to get to work unloading all this tea for you fine people to drink in the morning. So, if you'd please do us a kindness and clear the docks for us to move, we'd much appreciate it. Otherwise, I can't promise the little ones won't get squashed underfoot when we start hauling the crates about."

The crowd cheered him again, and then they began to disperse, but Cecil hung around. He had just enough sense not to get underfoot while the sailors were working, but he could not resist concealing himself behind a crate and watching the men work to unload their precious cargo. China, he thought with excitement, as he saw the wooden crates, lifted from the ship with pulleys and ropes. These boxes had come all the way from China. He could hardly imagine what such a faraway place must be like. Old Joe down at the market had been from China originally, and he told Cecil stories of a land filled with gold buildings and dragons flying in the sky, dragons like giant flying snakes, Old Joe always clarified, not dragons like you think of them, but Cecil was not entirely sure if he believed all of Old Joe's stories.

But one day, Cecil was determined, he would travel there himself, and then he would see the truth of it. Ships sailed from the port in Bristol all the time, to every place Cecil could imagine and many that he could not, and they always needed crewmen. Cecil's ma told him that he wasn't yet big or strong enough to join them, but Cecil was determined that he would grow. He would become so strong that the captains would have no choice but to take him on. He'd be so strong that the captains would fight over who could employ him. And then he, too, would sail the seas and see monstrous whales and terrifying sharks, would ride the waves of a storm, and see far off lands where everything was different except the sky.

But that day had not yet come, and Cecil was pulled out of his reverie when a firm hand gripped his arm, making him jump.

"Cecil Fontaine!" his mother shouted, loud enough that a few sailors glanced over to see the source of the noise. "What do you think you are doing out here?"

Cecil looked up at his mother's furious face. She was tall, or so Cecil thought, with a thin face and knowing brown eyes. Her fine brown hair pulled back into a practical bun, and the apron she wore over her dress was smeared with dirt.

"I'm watching the boats, Ma!" Cecil exclaimed. "This one just came in from China."

"I don't care if it came in from the moon," his mother snapped, pulling on his arm and dragging him away. "You're supposed to be working with your uncle. How dare you run off like that?"

"But Ma," Cecil said, as a few of the sailors snickered behind him. "I needed to see the *Taeping*."

"What you need to do," his mother said, "is listen to what you're told. You think we wouldn't like to go where we like and see what we like? We would. But we all have to work, Cecil."

Cecil pulled a face when his mother was not looking, but in truth, he could not argue with her. Her words sounded harsh, but Cecil was old enough to understand that money was a rare and precious thing for their family, and not a single penny could be passed up on. If Cecil was not at his uncle's shop, that meant his uncle could serve less customers, which meant less money for the family, which meant his mother and uncle wearing tired, stressed expressions as they tried to figure out how to pay the rent for that week and feed all five members of the family.

But this was exactly why Cecil went to the docks. Sailors made a fair amount of money. The riches they brought back sold for good prices, and the ships' owners were willing to pay decently to get their hands on as much tea or silk as possible. Sometimes the sailors could even get extra money if they made the journey particularly quick. And sailors did not often need to spend their wages, for they spent most of their time on the ship, with no food to buy or rent to pay. If Cecil became a sailor, he could earn a good amount of money, and send almost all of it to his mother and sisters, so they could live a better life too. And if Cecil wanted a place on a boat as soon as he possibly could, he needed to know his way around the docks. He needed to watch and learn from the sailors, so he could jump up and be impossibly useful from the very moment he finally stepped aboard as a crewman himself.

Cecil's mother did not consider this a worthwhile excuse. May Fontaine had been widowed at a young age, after her husband died in an accident unloading freight from the docks, and it terrified her to think of her small boy lingering there underfoot, possibly unseen, possibly in harm's way. May Fontaine was only twenty-seven, and the mother of four children, of whom Cecil was the oldest. Her younger daughters, Mary, Anne, and Jane, were all too small to bring in much of an income, but Cecil was a good worker when he put his mind to it, and the extra coins he earned could be the difference between making rent and being unable to pay. Of course, she wished that her son could follow his dreams and watch the ships for as long as he liked, but the reality of their situation would not allow it.

May Fontaine kept a small garden behind the house, where she grew vegetables and herbs to sell, as well as doing what washing and mending she could, but the family's main income came from her brother's work as a cobbler. After her husband's death, May Fontaine and her four children had moved in with her brother, Acker Wayne, whose own wife had died in childbirth, along with the babe, not a year before. They lived in a small three-room apartment above his shop near the docks, and together, they got by.

May dragged Cecil all the way to his uncle's cobbler shop and shoved him through the door. "Here," she said. "You'll never guess where I found him."

"By the docks?" Uncle Acker asked. "Watching that tea clipper come in?"

"The very same," May said. "If running off and watching ships earned someone a living, we'd be the richest family in England, I swear we would." She shook her head in frustration. "I have to get back upstairs," she said. "Mary is watching the little ones, but I shouldn't leave her for long. You," she added, pointing at her son. "Behave!"

As soon as she was gone, Cecil turned sheepishly to his uncle. Uncle Acker was not usually the sort to beat him for his disobedience, but if he had lost custom due to Cecil's absence, that was a completely different story. But Uncle Acker only smiled.

"You'll be the death of your mother, boy," he said, "if you don't start doing what you're told. She worries, you know. It's a strain on her poor heart."

That was almost worse than being beaten. "I know," Cecil said, looking at his feet. "I'm sorry. But," he couldn't help adding, "it came all the way from China."

"And soon it will go off to China again," Uncle Acker said. "And in the meantime, we'll have a lot of work to do."

"Do you think many of the sailors will bring their shoes in this time, Uncle Acker?"

"I couldn't say," Uncle Acker said. "Those sailors that need shoes fixed will, and if you promise to stay close at hand, I'll let you serve the customers and ask them as many pesky questions about life at sea as you like."

"Any questions I want?" Cecil asked.

"Anything you want," his uncle agreed. "But we won't get any sailors in if we don't do good work, so come on. I've got a pile of mended boots that all need polishing by you before their owners come back."

CHAPTER TWO

To Cecil's disappointment, no crewmember of *The Taeping* came by his uncle's shop that day, but his uncle kept him running around all day, and by the time he and his uncle shut the shop for the day and headed upstairs, he was exhausted.

His mother had not entirely forgiven him for his rebellion. "I hope you worked hard today, Cecil," she said, as he settled down for supper, and she narrowed her eyes suspiciously at him as he nodded in agreement.

His two youngest sisters, Anne and Jane, were already curled up asleep in their room, but seven-year-old Mary was awake, doing some mending for their ma. If Cecil was the rebellious one of the family, then Mary was the angel, always working hard, always desperate to please. It never occurred to Cecil to wonder if his sister was happy playing the role of a miniature mother to her family. He simply saw a girl who always seemed to please their mother without any effort or hardship at all, and the thought always made him feel bitter.

"How was the ship?" Mary asked him now, over her own dinner. "Was it very big?"

"Huge!" Cecil said. "Bigger than the town hall, I reckon." It was nowhere near that big, and Cecil thought his younger sister rather silly for believing it, when everybody knew that tea clippers had to be small and light to make their way through the ocean so quickly. Still, although Cecil deeply loved his sister, he could not resist teasing her sometimes, and allowing himself to feel a little superior when their mother so often implied that she was the good one of the pair.

"Don't tell stories," their ma said to him now. "A ship that big couldn't sail."

"It's not a story!" Cecil insisted. "It is that big. I saw it!"

"Hmm," was all his mother said. "Well, since you got to see it, it's your job to wash all the dishes tonight, and to sweep the floor before you go to bed."

"But Ma!" he exclaimed, but she cut him off.

"But nothing, Cecil," she said. "I'm still angry with you for that stunt you pulled. You can't go running off like that again."

Cecil had no intention of never running off like that to see the ships again, but he made the effort now to look contrite. Perhaps it was the knowledge that he fully intended to break his word to his mother and return to the docks again, but he completed his extra chores without complaint, before finally settling down in the corner of the front room to sleep.

Their apartment only had three rooms, so it was a little impractical for a family of six, but they got by as best they could. May Fontaine shared one room with her three daughters, and Uncle Acker, as the man of the house and the main earner, slept in the other, smaller room alone. That left the front room for Cecil to sleep in, but Cecil did not mind overly much. He slept not far from the stove, so there was always some lingering heat in the room after dinner, and the walls muffled some of his family's snores. It was the only time of day when he ever got to be completely alone, and although he loved his family very much, Cecil also appreciated the quiet and the chance to be alone with his thoughts. As he drifted to sleep that night, his mind was full of adventures on ships and a far-off land made of gold, where dragons soared through the sky.

A few streets away, in the dock's slums, an eight-year-old girl also dreamed of ships and China. Samantha Cole had gone to bed hungry that night, as she did most nights, for the weekly rent had been due, and she and her mother had no coins to spare for food.

Despite the emptiness in her stomach, Samantha felt that she had had an exciting day. She sold flowers to passers-by for money, and her ma had allowed her to go down near the docks to try and sell to the crowds that gathered to see the ship from China sail in. With blonde curls and big blue eyes, Samantha Cole was very good at plucking at passers-by's heartstrings and convincing them to bring a flower home to their mother or wife, but she had been distracted that day by the strange, arrow-like shape of the ship that arrived and its huge number of billowing sails. Unlike Cecil, Samantha had no hope of dreaming to one day be a crew member on such a ship herself, but she still loved the romance of them, and loved to imagine all the wonders that the ship and her crew had seen.

Sadly, life left Samantha with little time for dreaming. Her father had died six months before, and her grieving mother Susan was overcome by grief. Samantha had to try her best to earn money for the pair of them, to prepare food, and to make sure that rent was paid so they were not thrown out onto the streets. They had not been able to afford their own house, but even the one-room space they had moved into a month prior was almost impossible to afford, and although her mother had since come back to herself and started working harder than ever to support them both, Samantha still felt like she was now personally responsible for her family's wellbeing and survival. Unlike

Cecil, she did not dream of an adventurous future. She only thought of tomorrow, and how to get food on the table by the end of the day.

But that night, taken in by the romance of *The Taeping*, she dared to dream of something more.

The following morning was cold and overcast, a miserable mid-October day, and Samantha wrapped her worn shawl tightly around her shoulders before heading out. She held a basket of flowers in one hand and a single stem in the other, and she looked up at every passer-by with an imploring face.

"Buy a flower," she said. "Please buy a flower. Sir, would you buy a flower? Please?"

Most passers-by ignored her. The sky was threatening rain, and the chill in the air meant that everyone was eager to reach their destination as quickly as possible. But the weather would only get colder and wetter as winter drew in, and if Samantha could not sell flowers now, she would be doomed when January came. So, she flexed her stiff fingers to keep them warm and continued to wander the streets, holding out flowers to everyone she saw who looked even vaguely rich.

Around lunchtime, the heavens suddenly opened, and rain pounded onto the pavement. It was so hard and so sudden that Samantha squealed in shock and gaped in horror as her basket of flowers was soaked through in an instant. She ran and hid under the overhang of a nearby building, shaking water out of her blonde locks.

All around her, other people also shouted and ran for cover. Samantha watched them scatter and struggled not to cry. She wouldn't sell a single flower if the rain continued. She might perhaps go to the covered market, but the real flower sellers also worked there. The grown-ups with stalls and a range of blooms for sale would get angry if they saw Samantha wandering around selling her goods for a penny a stem. Last time she had gone there, one of the stallholders had even called over a policeman, and Samantha had had to scramble out of the building as fast as her small legs could carry her and hide in an alleyway to avoid getting in trouble. It might be worth the risk to go back, though, if the other option was another evening without anything to eat.

While she was considering, the door of the shop behind her opened, and a skinny boy about her age stepped out. He had messy brown hair and shoe polish staining his hands. He looked down past the overhang over the building at the raindrops bouncing off the pavement.

"Cecil!" a man's voice shouted from inside. "What're you doing?"

"Look at the rain!" Cecil said. "It's like a monsoon!"

Samantha had never heard that word 'monsoon' before, so she could not have said whether his statement was true.

"A monsoon, eh?" the man inside said.

"Yes, a monsoon," the boy repeated. "Captain Rupert told me about them! He said they hit in the summer in India and places like that, and if you're not careful, the rain could near wash a man away."

"Did he now?" the man inside replied. "Come inside and shut the door, lad. You're letting all the cold in."

Cecil gaped for another long moment at the rain, and then turned to return inside and spotted Samantha. "How'd'y do?" he said to her. "My name's Cecil."

"I'm Samantha," Samantha said.

"Cecil!" the voice inside shouted again.

"That's my Uncle Acker," Cecil said.

"Oh," Samantha said. "Right."

Cecil looked Samantha up and down, taking in her soaked dress and bedraggled hair. "You should come in too," he said. "Get dry. It's pretty warm in there. Well, it was, til I opened the door, I guess."

"Oh, no, I couldn't," Samantha said. She picked up her skirt with the hand holding a single flower. "I'm soaked through."

"So, you should come in and warm up," Cecil said decidedly. "Come on." He strode back through the door, and then waited for Samantha to follow.

Good manners told Samantha that she should not go inside and drip water all over the shop floor, but they also dictated that she should not bluntly refuse an invitation, and as she was fair shivering from the rain by that point, it was that second compulsion that won out. She smiled nervously at Cecil and stepped past him into the cosy warmth of the shop.

A man in his thirties with messy brown hair, just like Cecil's, sat working at a desk. He was hammering nails into the sole of a leather boot, but he paused to watch the two of them enter. "Who's this, now?" he asked.

"This is Samantha," Cecil said, in a tone that brooked no argument.

Uncle Acker smiled at her. "Not a good day to be selling flowers," he said. "Might as well stay in here with us 'til the rain stops. No one else will be walking around for a while."

Samantha nodded. She hesitated for a moment, and then sat down on one of the wooden stools placed near the door. Cecil sat down beside her.

"I haven't seen you before," Cecil said. "Where are you from?"

Samantha did not want to admit she lived in the slums, so she just shrugged. "My ma and I live near the docks," she said. "We just moved here a month ago."

"I live here," Cecil said. "Well, up there," he added, pointing at the ceiling.

"Cecil," Uncle Acker said suddenly. "Why don't you buy a flower or two for your ma? To say sorry for what happened yesterday, hm? Worrying her and all?"

"Ma doesn't like me going down to the docks to see the ships," Cecil confided to Samantha. "But I had to go yesterday and see the *Taeping*. It had just come all the way from China."

"*The Taeping?*" Samantha repeated. "Was it that funny-looking pointy ship that came yesterday?"

"It's not funny-looking," Cecil insisted. "It's the fastest ship in the whole world."

"Now don't tell lies, Cecil," Uncle Acker said, but Cecil shook his head insistently.

"It's true!" he said. "Captain Rupert told me!"

"And Captain Rupert would never lie."

"He wouldn't!" Cecil said.

Uncle Acker just chuckled. "Either way," he said. "I think your ma would appreciate a flower, don't you?"

Cecil looked somewhat doubtfully at the basket of flowers in Samantha's hand. "They're all wet," he said.

"They're flowers, boy! They survive a bit of rain all the time. Now come over here and take a shilling."

"Oh, they're only a penny each," Samantha said, but Uncle Acker did not listen. He handed a shiny coin over to his nephew, and Cecil solemnly returned to Samantha's side and passed the coin to her. She tried to give him several flowers in return, but Uncle Acker was insistent.

"They're such pretty flowers," he said. "One is certainly worth a shilling." And when Samantha imagined what food that shilling could buy, her hand closed around it almost involuntarily, and she found herself unable to argue again.

The rain soon calmed, leaving large dirty puddles on the street and a little bit of weak sunshine, fighting its way through the clouds. A couple of people began to venture out again, and soon Samantha needed to leave and return to work too. She gave Cecil and Uncle Acker a heart-felt thank you, but she felt so embarrassed and awkward in light of their generosity that she scurried away quickly, finding another street to work.

"Why'd you insist on giving her a shilling, Uncle Acker?" Cecil asked, after the girl had gone. "Ma'll be furious we wasted money."

"No, lad," Uncle Acker said. "You think we struggle sometimes? That was what real poverty looks like. That girl hadn't eaten properly in far too long. That money will do her far more good than it'll do us, and your ma would think the same."

"Then why didn't you just give it to her?" Cecil asked.

"Just because someone is struggling," Uncle Acker said, "doesn't mean they're willing to accept help or charity from strangers. That was a proud girl if I ever saw one. Try and give her some money, and she'd refuse it. So, we buy a flower, and everyone is happy. Besides, your ma will like it. Just tell her it was your idea, not mine, alright?"

"Because she'll be angry?" Cecil said cautiously.

"Because she'll be thankful, you foolish boy," Uncle Acker chuckled. "Now come away from the door. We're got a lot of work left to do before we can close for the day."

CHAPTER THREE

Cecil's mother beamed and hugged him when he gave her the flower, and she wore it tucked behind her ear for the rest of that day and all of the next. Cecil kept an eye out for Samantha, in case she appeared outside the shop again, but he saw no sign of her, and soon another distraction came to drive her from his mind.

Captain Rupert's ship, *The Queen Victoria*, arrived in the docks from its latest journey to India, and although Cecil did not manage to sneak away to watch its arrival, he knew that the captain would visit the shop very soon. Captain Rupert always went to Uncle Acker for any shoes that needed repairing, and he and Uncle Acker had become quite good friends over the years. Captain Rupert had something of a soft spot for Cecil as well, and always brought the boy stories and tiny treasures from his travels abroad.

Cecil spent the entire rest of the day peering through the window whenever he could, desperately hoping to see the captain approach, but it was not until the following morning that he glimpsed the man striding down the street through the autumn mist.

Cecil yelped in excitement and ran to the door, and even Uncle Acker paused with what he was doing to chuckle at his nephew's antics and smile at his approaching friend through the window. Captain Rupert Bright was a seasoned sailor, fifty years old with salt and pepper hair and a sailor's beard. He had lost one of his arms in a sailing accident many years before, although every time Cecil asked him what had happened, he told a completely different story, each one more ridiculous and grizzlier than the last. Cecil's favourite tale was that it had been bitten off while he was wrestling a shark that had leapt on deck to devour the crew, but he was always eager to hear what else the captain could come up with. Every story, he thought, must have some sliver of truth to them, some hint of a real thing that happened to real sailors at sea, and so he was hungry for every tale he could get, no matter how tall it might seem.

Captain Rupert always said that losing his arm had made him particularly value his three remaining limbs, and that the most important thing to keep your legs in good working order was a good pair of shoes. This meant he visited the cobbler's as regularly as his ship came into

Bristol docks, making him one of Uncle Acker's best customers.

"Ahoy there, cap'n," Cecil said, saluting the man as he came through the door.

Captain Rupert chuckled. "Ahoy there, sailor," he said. "Morning, Acker, my friend," he added to Uncle Acker.

"Rupert!" Uncle Acker exclaimed. "Glad to see you back in one piece again."

"Well, the sharks did try to have a bite at me," he said to Cecil with a wink, "but this old seadog is much too quick for them these days."

"What can I do for you today?" Uncle Acker asked.

"These boots," Captain Rupert said, gesturing at his feet. "They are letting in water, which ain't so convenient when you're a sailor. And the sole is peeling off a bit too. Think you can fix it for me today?"

"Can do," Uncle Acker said. "Hand 'em over here and I'll give them a look."

Cecil hovered by Captain Rupert's side as his uncle assessed the shoes and took Captain Rupert's payment. Since Captain Rupert had handed over the very shoes he was wearing, he had no choice but to sit on one of the stools by the door to wait, and the moment he was seated, Cecil ran over to him and began peppering him with questions. It never would have occurred to Cecil that a well-off man like Captain Rupert must own more than one pair of shoes, and that the captain had worn his broken boots on purpose, so he had an excuse to stay and talk.

"What did you bring back this time?" Cecil asked him. "Jewels? Gold?"

Captain Rupert laughed. "Not quite, lad," he said. "Rubber, mostly."

"Oh," Cecil said. Rubber was not very exciting to hear about. "Anything else?"

"Some tea," Captain Rupert said. "Some spices. There's one that's bright orange. Get within five feet of it and it'll stain your hands and not wash off for love nor money, so I reckon we should coat all our crates with it, to deter any thieves."

"But then wouldn't you become orange too?" Cecil asked.

"I would," Captain Rupert said. "But I'm an old man, lad. I'm not fussed over how I look, like these young things today."

"What about elephants?" Cecil asked, remembering the stories Captain Rupert had shared after his last visit to India, of creatures the size of carriages with long noses that they used like an extra arm. "Did you see any this time?"

"A couple," Captain Rupert said. "They're strong beasts, they are, much stronger than our horses, though more like to do real damage to you if they step on your toes or trample you down. They have 'em in pulleys at the docks, hauling freight. Makes it much quicker than doing it without, as long as the beasts behave."

"Do they always behave?"

"Always when I've seen 'em," Captain Rupert said. "But beasts are beasts. You've seen horses, lad. Even the best of them can get spooked occasionally. These elephants are just the same, except you really don't want to be around when it happens."

Cecil tried to imagine it. The hot humid air, the faces of people whose lives were so different from his own, men riding elephants and using them to haul cargo off the boats. He imagined elephants on the roads, pulling carriages the way horses did in England, but if elephants were so big, they must be able to pull huge carriages. Could one elephant pull a whole autobus by itself? Could it pull a train?

"I can't wait to go," Cecil said. "Will you take me with you next time?"

"Now see here, lad," Captain Rupert said fondly. "The sea's a dangerous place, as I've told you, what with the shark wrestling an' all. It's not the place for a young thing like you. Might be I'll take you on when you're older, but for now, you stay home with your ma and uncle and help them out, you hear?"

Cecil could not help feeling a little disappointed, even though he had already known what the answer would be. Captain Rupert might allow him to sail one day, but *one day* was not for what felt like a very long time yet. Still, Cecil nodded, and Captain Rupert ruffled his hair. "Good lad," he said. "Now, then. Why don't you tell me what I've missed here, eh? Your ma still keeping well?"

Cecil launched into the tales of all his adventures in the six months since he had seen Captain Rupert last, and his sadness was soon forgotten.

Captain Rupert was not just a loyal customer, but also a well-paying one. He valued Uncle Acker's craftsmanship, and he was always extremely generous with his tips after returning from a long voyage at sea. Uncle Acker was so pleased with the pay that he called Cecil over after Captain Rupert had left and pressed three shiny pennies into his hand.

"Why don't you run to the shop on the corner," he said, "and pick us both up some of those boiled sweets? As many as you can get with this. Some of those pear drops, and maybe some liquorice, if they have some."

Cecil beamed at him. "Thanks, Uncle Acker!" he said, and Uncle Acker ruffled his hair.

"Go on with you," he said. "And watch yourself crossing the street. Your ma'd never forgive me if you got hit by a carriage." Cecil was already running out the door. "And come straight back!" Uncle Acker shouted after him. "No dallying! And don't even think of going to the docks!"

But for once, Cecil did not have ships in his thoughts. The rare treat of sweets from the shop on the corner was delight enough to distract him entirely, and although visiting the docks was worth facing many punishments, it was not worth never being treated to a paper bag of boiled sweets and liquorice again.

Cecil forgot to check the street before running across it, so it was lucky that the road was quiet. He careened along the pavement towards the gleaming glass windows of the sweet shop, his eyes fixed on the many glass jars crammed full of brightly coloured sweets. But before he reached it, he noticed a familiar girl standing outside it, clutching a basket of flowers.

It was Samantha, the skinny blonde girl who had come into the shop from the rain. She was holding out flowers to passers-by, begging them to buy them, but most people were ignoring her.

Cecil paused, feeling the weight of the coins in his hand. He had not been allowed sweets for weeks, and his uncle was looking forward to the treat too. Uncle Acker might be angry if he used the money for any other purpose. But the girl looked so thin and forlorn. Cecil wondered when the last time she had eaten was. He had gone hungry occasionally, usually as a punishment from his ma rather than from any real scarcity of food, and he hated the way it made his stomach ache. He could not imagine what it must be like to never have enough food, no matter what you dd.

His mind made up, he approached the girl. "Hullo," he said to her, and she turned to him and gave him a shy smile.

"Hello," she said. "You're the boy from the cobbler's."

"That I am," he said. "And you're the girl with the flowers."

Samantha gave him a small, joking curtsey in response.

"I'd like to buy some," Cecil said quickly. "My ma, she loved the flower I got from you last time. I wanted to get another."

"Oh," Samantha said. "Did she really like it?"

"Yes," Cecil said. "It made her so happy."

Samantha smiled. "Here," she said, holding out the basket to him. "You can pick another one if you like."

Cecil carefully considered the blooms and plucked out a pretty white one for his ma. Then he pressed all three coins into Samantha's tiny hand.

"It's only a penny per flower," Samantha said softly.

"But I took the prettiest one," Cecil said. "So, I think it's worth three."

Uncle Acker looked surprised when Cecil returned a few minutes later carrying a single flower and with no sweets in sight, but when Cecil explained what had happened, he was not angry. Quite the opposite, in fact.

"You're a good lad, Cecil," he said. "Kind-hearted, like your ma. Well," he added, considering his drawer of takings from the day. "I think we can spare another couple of pennies to get a treat, don't you? Take this and get a bag and go share them with that girl. Don't come back until they're all gone, you hear?"

"Thank you, Uncle Acker!" Cecil gushed, and without another word, he snatched the coins from his uncle's hand and raced out of the door.

CHAPTER FOUR

Samantha had wanted to thank the cobblers for their kindness, but her shyness overruled the impulse, and she had been unable to go back to the store. She was certain they had already forgotten all about her anyway. To them, she had just been a poor girl selling flowers in the rain, even though to her they were the people who allowed her and her ma to eat that night.

So, Samantha was both nervous and delighted when the boy, Cecil, called out to her to buy another bloom. She was even more surprised when Cecil came running back not five minutes later, holding his clenched fist out in front of him like it contained a great prize.

"Uncle Acker gave us money for sweets!" he said. "Come on."

Samantha knew that she should argue. She did not know this boy or his uncle, and she shouldn't be accepting food from them. But sweets! She had not eaten a single sweet since her father died. She had chosen to stand in this spot solely because it allowed her to peer in through the shop's windows and imagine herself eating the treats within. She would give so much to be able to have even one single boiled sweet, but she and her ma did not have even a penny to spare.

Cecil grabbed her hand and rushed onward, toward the sweet shop's door, and with the promise of sugar so close, Samantha found herself unable to protest.

The little bell above the shop door rang as they entered, and a plump middle-aged woman looked up from behind the desk and smiled at them. "Welcome, dears," she said. "What would you like?"

Cecil held out the coins. "How much can we get for this?"

The next few minutes were filled with the two children directing the lady about what sweets to put in their large paper bag. Cecil insisted that Samantha offer her opinion, and the pink and yellow sweets were just too tempting for her to resist. They ended up with a bag of fruit drops, pear and lemon and rhubarb and apple, along with some orange barley sugars and even one large stick jaw toffee each. They also got a small bag of liquorice and Pontefract cakes for Uncle Acker, and then they scurried outside the shop to eat their treasures.

They sat on the pavement directly outside the shop, and although Samantha could feel the owner looking at them through the window, she did not come outside and shoo them away. Cecil plucked a barley sugar from the bag and popped it into his mouth before offering the open bag to Samantha. She reached in tentatively and pulled out a pink pear drop. She slipped it into her mouth too, and then closed her eyes and smiled in delight as the sugar hit her tongue.

"So good," Cecil said, around the sweet. "I haven't had any barley sugars in weeks."

"I haven't had any in months," Samantha admitted quietly. "We can't afford 'em. Can't really afford anything these days."

"Do you live with your ma and pa?" Cecil asked.

"My ma," Samantha said, hugging her knees to her chest. "My pa is gone to Heaven."

"Mine too," Cecil said. "I have my ma, though. And my Uncle Acker. He takes care of us. Where's your ma now?"

"At home," Samantha said. "She doesn't leave much. Most of the time, she stays in bed." She could feel Cecil looking at her, and she imagined the pity and judgement on his face. "It's not her fault," she added forcefully. "She's been different since pa died. I think, I think maybe part of her died with him, and now she can't do anything."

Cecil said nothing, and Samantha closed her eyes, focusing on the sweetness of the pear drop. She wanted to make it last as long as possible.

"Come on," Cecil said after a moment. He stood and held out a hand to Samantha. "Let's go to the docks. I bet there's some big interesting ship in port that we can look at. When I'm sad, I always go to the docks, and the boats always make me feel better."

Samantha could not see how a strange ship might make any difference to the situation with her mother, but Cecil looked so earnest that she did not want to argue. Besides, she thought, as she took his hand and he pulled her to her feet. She had enjoyed seeing the ship from China a couple of weeks before, hadn't she? It had given her something else to dream of as she struggled to get to sleep.

The pair scrambled up onto a low wall near the docks, overlooking the sea. A couple of ships were in port, and another was sailing on the horizon. Cecil pointed at each one and explained their origin. This one was from the Americas, which one could tell from the stars on the flag, while that one was just a local ship, probably heading around the south coast.

"I'm going to be a sailor," Cecil said, "when I'm older. Then I'll travel all around the world."

"I wish I could see the world," Samantha said softly. As she watched the ships, she imagined what it would be like to be anywhere other than here, if she ran away from this life and its hunger and the sadness she felt every time she looked at her ma, and turned to adventure instead.

"You should sail too!" Cecil said.

Samantha shook her head. "I don't think girls can sail."

"Well, not as girls," Cecil said. "But girls dress up as boys and work on ships all the time."

Samantha gave him a disbelieving look. "They do not," she said.

"They do!" Cecil insisted. "I've read about it!"

"In stories," Samantha said. "Stories aren't real."

"No, in real life too!" Cecil said. "There was a lady pirate in the Americas. More than one! So, you could at least be a pirate, which is probably more fun than being a regular sailor anyway."

"Don't let them hear you," Samantha said, "or they'll never take you on. They'll be too scared you'll turn rogue."

"Nah," Cecil said. "My charm will win them over." He plucked another sweet out of the bag. "Captain Rupert has promised me a place on his ship when I'm older. I just have to wait 'til then."

Samantha nodded and said nothing. She could not help feeling a spike of jealousy at Cecil's confident words. She couldn't see any future for herself. Tomorrow would be exactly like today, and the day after that, and the day after that, until she and her ma ran out of money, and got thrown out on the streets.

"You look sad," Cecil said. "What's wrong?"

To Samantha's surprise, she realised she had tears in her eyes. She wiped them with the back of her hand and shook her head. "Nothing," she said. "I'm alright."

"You're crying," Cecil insisted. "That's not nothing."

Samantha sniffed. "I just miss my pa," she said. "And my ma too. I wish I could go away."

"Maybe I can talk to Captain Rupert," he said. "He might hire you, too!"

"I can't leave my ma," Samantha said. "She needs me."

"Then I'll go, and I'll tell you so much about it that it'll be like you went, too," Cecil declared. "And I'll bring you presents back too. Gifts that will make you rich! Flowers from China and perfume from the Near East and an elephant from India."

"An elephant?" Samantha repeated. "How will you get it on the ship?"

"I'll ask it nicely," Cecil said, and Samantha could not help but laugh.

Cecil left Samantha with the rest of the pear drops, and she stored them carefully in her pocket to bring home to her ma. Perhaps they would cheer her up. She continued to try and sell flowers until it got dark, and the sweets seemed to have given her good luck, because she managed to empty her basket before it was time to turn for home. She used half the coins to pick up some food for her and her ma, saving the other half for the rent, and made her way through the slums to the one-room cottage she shared with her ma.

She was surprised and pleased to find her ma sitting up at the table, doing a little mending. She proudly handed over the food, and then revealed the bag of sweets from her pocket.

But her ma was not pleased. "Where did you get these, Sam?" she asked. "We can't afford these!"

"They were a gift, mama," Samantha said. "A friend gave them to me."

"A friend?" her ma asked, eyes narrowed. "What friend?"

"The boy at the cobbler's," Samantha said. "Cecil Fontaine. He was going to the sweet shop to buy some sweets and he offered me some too."

"You shouldn't accept gifts like that from people, Samantha," her mother snapped. She pressed the heels of her hands against her eyes, sighing. "We cannot be in debt to anyone else."

"It was just a gift, ma."

"Nothing is just a gift," her ma said. "Don't you forget it."

Samantha wanted to cry again, but she managed to hold back her tears. Her mother barely ever spoke to her except to berate her these days, and of course, the one time ma was alert enough to worry about money would be the day Samantha had actually done something that made her happy. She thought Cecil might be the sweetest boy she had ever met. She really hoped they would get to spend time with one another again. But she also could not bear to make her mother upset.

"I'm sorry, Ma," Samantha said. "I thought you'd like them."

Her mother sighed. "No," she said. "I'm sorry, Sammie. I just have a bit of a headache. Make some dinner for us, would you?"

And Samantha could do nothing except comply.

Samantha and Cecil saw each other almost every day after that. Uncle Acker started buying bunches of flowers to display in the showroom, to give it a more welcoming, homey feel, he claimed, and found excuses to bring Samantha inside when the weather was bad. Samantha loved watching Cecil and Uncle Acker working on shoes, and she loved hearing them talk too.

Soon, Cecil's mother learned about Samantha, and she too began to come downstairs occasionally, finding excuses to give Samantha leftover food or herbs and vegetables from her garden. "Oh, they're such a strange shape," May

Fontaine, said, holding out a few carrots. "You know what rich people are like. It's perfectly good, but they won't buy it unless it's perfect, so I can't sell it. And I can't stand eating carrots myself. Please, take it."

Samantha was no fool. She knew what they were all doing for her, and she appreciated it deeply. As her mother gained strength, they moved out of the desperate poverty they had once been in, as her mother could work a little and earn money too, but she would still have often been hungry without the Fontaines' support. She began to think of Uncle Acker and Aunt May, as she called Cecil's mother, as her family too, and when her heart hurt too much for her to bear it, she would go and sit in their kitchen and play with Cecil's little sisters, or sit near the docks with Cecil and watch the ships go by.

CHAPTER FIVE

Soon after Cecil's thirteenth birthday, Captain Rupert returned from another trip and went straight to Uncle Acker's shop. Cecil was taller now than he had been at age nine, but was still somewhat scrawny, with an uncontrollable mop of brown hair. He had learned enough, in the years that had passed, to know not to immediately jump at Captain Rupert for stories when he came to shore, but he could not stop himself grinning when the bell above the door rang and he saw the familiar man walking inside.

"Didn't know you'd be back today," Cecil said. "I thought it was next week."

"We made good time," Captain Rupert said. "Is your uncle around? Need a word with him."

"He's in the back," Cecil said. "I'll fetch him."

But Uncle Acker had already appeared in the doorway. "Rupert!" he cried. "Good to see you."

"You too, Acker," Captain Rupert said. "Can I have a word, though? Maybe with May too, if she's around."

"Of course," Uncle Acker said, looking a little confused, and he led Captain Rupert into the back office.

Cecil had to work very hard to remain at his worktable and not attempt to eavesdrop on the conversation. He was burning with curiosity, but he knew he had to always make a good impression on Captain Rupert if he ever wanted a chance of joining his crew.

His uncle and Captain Rupert were ensconced in the back room for at least half an hour, and Cecil grew more and more fidgety as the time passed. What could they possibly be talking about? But eventually, Captain Rupert and his uncle reappeared, and both of them were smiling.

"Well, then, lad," Captain Rupert said. "Turns out I'm going to be starting on a new ship, and I'm in need of a cabin boy. I think thirteen's finally old enough to start learning the ropes of sailing, so to speak, don't you? Now your uncle and your ma have both given permission for you to join me, if that's still what you want. So, would you like a job, lad?"

Cecil knew he was grinning so widely, his face might be at risk of splitting in two. He was so overjoyed that he could barely speak. "Really, sir?" he said eventually. "Do you mean it?"

"Of course, I mean it!" Captain Rupert said. "I always said I'd get you a spot when the time was right, now, didn't I? Well, now the time is right."

"Thank you!" Cecil said. "I won't let you down, sir, I promise!"

"It's just 'Cap'n' now," Captain Rupert said, "since you'll be on the crew."

"Yes, Cap'n," Cecil said, and Captain Rupert laughed.

"We'll be setting off in about a week," Captain Rupert said. "It's a ship called the Santa Lucia, a passenger liner. We'll be taking people between here and the Americas, and we'll be carrying some goods beside. Maybe not the big adventure you were hoping for, lad, but it's a good place to start. I'll have a crew of over a hundred men."

Although Cecil had dreams of travelling on a tea clipper to the East, he would have accepted any job if it meant finally getting to sail. He was so excited that he could hardly concentrate on his work for the rest of the day, and Uncle Acker gently scolded him for sloppy work several times before giving up and telling him to go out and burn off his energy somewhere else and come back when he was ready to be useful again.

Cecil immediately set out to find Sam and tell her the good news. In the three years that Cecil had known Sam, her life had improved greatly. Her mother still had dark moments, but she was rarely confined to her bed any more, and the two worked together buying fish cheaply from the fishermen on the dockside and then frying it and selling it to workers from their small food stall.

Sam's mother Susan was not very fond of Cecil, for reasons that Cecil had never quite been able to figure out, but she never forbade their friendship. Still, Cecil would rather avoid seeing her if he possibly could, so he was relieved to see Sam standing alone behind the food stall when he arrived.

"Cecil!" she said with a grin when she saw him. "I didn't know if I'd see you today."

When they had been a little younger, Cecil had greeted Samantha with a hug, but his mother had a word with him a year ago about how they were both growing older, and about what was and was not proper for little adults, and Cecil had to learn to refrain. Sam had grown into a very pretty girl. She had more roundness about her cheeks since she started eating properly again, and her blue eyes had a lively spark to them, where they had been dull before.

"I've got big news!" he said. "Captain Rupert just spoke to Uncle Acker. He has a job for me!"

"A job?" Sam asked. "On a ship?"

"Yes!" Cecil said. "On a huge liner. The Santa Lucia! He wants me to be his cabin boy. I'll be going to America."

"That's wonderful, Cecil," Sam said. "I'm so happy for you." She was smiling, but Cecil could not help noticing a hint of sadness in her eyes as she spoke.

"What's wrong, Sammie?" he asked. "Do you not want me to go?'

"No," Sam said, "of course I want you to go. I want you to be happy. I'll just—I'm going to miss you, that's all."

"I won't be gone forever," Cecil said. "I'll still be in Bristol half the year, and I'll finally be able to bring back all the things I promised you."

"Like the elephant?" Sam asked.

"Elephant?" Cecil said. "I never promised you an elephant."

"You did!" Sam insisted. "I remember it distinctly. It was one of the first times we met. You said you'd coax an elephant onto the ship and bring it home for me, and then I'd be able to ride it around Bristol and trample anyone who looked meanly at me when I tried to sell my flowers."

"Alright, alright," Cecil said. "A promise is a promise."

"Good," Sam said, but after a moment, her smile faded slightly again. "You are going to have such adventures," she said. "But I will miss you. I don't know what I will do without seeing you every day."

"I'll miss you as well," Cecil said. "I wish you could come too."

"I'll chop off all my hair and disguise myself as a boy!" Sam said, but then she shook her head. "Even if that wasn't a foolish plan," she said, "Ma needs me here."

"Then you'll have to save up every bit of news that happens," Cecil said, "and tell me when I get back."

"It won't be as interesting as the stories you'll have to tell," Sam said.

"All your stories are interesting, Sammie," Cecil said.

A customer came up to the stall, and Sam was distracted for a moment preparing his fish. Cecil stood slightly to the side, watching her. Life without Sam around would be incredibly difficult to bear, but at least he could always trust that she would be here to see him every time he came back to port.

"Sammie," he said, after the customer had gone. "Don't leave Bristol, okay?"

"Why would I leave Bristol?" Sammie asked him.

"I don't know," Cecil said. "Maybe some rich duke will show up one day and become enchanted by your beauty and whisk you off to his manor to be his wife."

"A rich duke," Sam repeated, quirking one eyebrow at him.

"Stranger things have happened!" Cecil said. "If I was a rich duke, I know I'd fall in love with you." Cecil blushed as he realised what he had said, and Samantha's cheeks also turned a little pink as she smiled and turned away.

"I suppose you're lucky you're not a rich duke, then," she said.

"I am," Cecil agreed, "since I just told you not to go running off with one. Sammie." He paused and began fidgeting with his sleeve, unsure what to say. "I'm going to make my fortune. You'll see. And once I do, I'll come back, pet elephant and all, and give it all to you."

"Don't be silly, Cecil," Sam said. "It's your fortune."

"It'll be our fortune," he said. "One day, I'll be rich and grown and I'll ask you to marry me, and I hope you'll say yes. So, don't be too sad that I'm going, alright?"

Samantha was determinedly not looking at him, but her smile was even bigger now. "Well," she said. "If that's the case, I suppose I might be tempted to accept."

"Good," Cecil said, his face bright red now. "Good. That's good."

Still, Cecil could not resist asking his mother to take extra good care of Samantha while he was away. Sitting at the dinner table in the kitchen above the shop, sharing a meal of vegetables and fried fish from Samantha's stall, Cecil's mother gave him an exaggerated scowl.

"As though I'd do anything different," she said. "That girl is like family. 'Take care of Samantha'. Who do you think I am, Cecil?"

"Will you bring me back a present?" little six-year-old Jane asked her older brother.

"Of course," he said. "What would you like?"

Jane looked thoughtful for a moment. "A shark's tooth!" she said. "Or a mermaid's scale. Or the severed leg of someone who has been eaten by a shark! That one!"

"Jane!" their mother exclaimed. "I don't know where you get these ideas from. No one is getting eaten by a shark, and even if they were, your brother is not bringing part of them home. Really, my girl. You can't ask for a doll or a ribbon like a normal child?"

"Dolls and ribbons are boring," Jane said sulkily, and Uncle Acker laughed.

"You can't pretend to not know where she's got it from, either," he said. "She's been around Cecil and his tales of Captain Rupert her whole life. She'll be a little pirate yet."

The next few days were filled with the rush of preparation, as Cecil's mother ran around to ensure that he had enough warm clothes for the journey and Cecil packed and repacked the small bag he was allowed to take aboard with him. He and Samantha went down to the docks one morning just to look at the Santa Lucia, and Cecil was speechless and in awe. The Santa Lucia had sails, like every ship, but she was mainly a steam-powered liner, and large metal pipes stood between the masts. She was longer than most ships Cecil had ever seen, with an iron hull and a huge screw propeller to push her through the water. She looked grand and regal, nothing like the narrow trading ships that darted around the world, but Cecil thought he could be proud to call such a vessel his home. It wasn't the wild adventure that he had imagined, but it was a better start than most boys could dream of.

Finally, the day of his departure dawned. Cecil hauled his knapsack onto his shoulder and walked toward the docks with his family. Jane clung to his hand, peppering him with questions about the journey, while his mother kept fussing with the position of his collar and the tidiness of his hair.

Samantha met them at the docks with tears in her eyes, and she flung her arms around Cecil and held him tight.

"Don't worry, Sam," he said. "I'll be back before you know it."

Samantha nodded and sniffed and stepped back, and his mother embraced him. "Eat fruit," she said. "The doctors say sailors used to get sick because they didn't eat enough fruit, so eat all you can, alright? And be good. Stay away from the edge. Don't climb the masts. And do what the captain says."

"What if he tells me to climb the mast, Ma?" Cecil asked, and she cuffed him affectionately around the ear.

Then he was shaking hands with Uncle Acker. "You're a good lad," Uncle Acker said to him. "Make us proud."

Cecil promised that he would, and soon, too soon, Captain Rupert was there, insisting that it was time for all the crew to come aboard and prepare for departure. Cecil's mother gave him one final hug, and then Cecil was walking up the gangplank and onto his very own ship.

Cecil had no actual experience with sailing a steamship, and could contribute nothing with the big rush for departure, so Captain Rupert allowed him to stand by the railing, a little bit away from the rich ladies and gentlemen who were travelling on the ship, and join them in waving to his family as the ship pulled away from the dock.

"Goodbye, Cecil!" Sam shouted, and although the words were lost on the wind, Cecil could see her lips moving and knew she was shouting to him. "Be well!"

"Don't forget my sharks' teeth!" Jane shouted.

"Be good!" his mother cried. Cecil waved and waved, grinning broadly, as his family's teary faces faded into the distance and then disappeared from sight altogether.

CHAPTER SIX

Life on the Santa Lucia was both far more difficult and far more boring than Cecil had anticipated. As cabin boy, his duties basically involved doing absolutely anything that anyone told him to, and the captain and senior crew members had him running up and down the great ship at all hours of the day. He helped in the kitchens, preparing food for both the sailors and the passengers, and then carried the crew's meals from the kitchen to the forecastle where they all ate. He was responsible for keeping the captain's quarters clean and tidy, and also for cleaning anywhere else that anyone sent him. Apart from the fact that they were upon the sea, it did not really feel like being a sailor at all.

But Cecil was determined to make a good impression. If he worked hard, he knew that he could potentially progress to better jobs, but if he slacked off with these basic duties, he'd be dropped off back at Bristol and never chosen to work again. Lord Nelson had started off as a cabin boy, and Francis Drake. Although Cecil did not dare to dream that he would ever become an admiral, like Nelson, he knew that this was just the beginning of his sailing career, and he had to do the very best he could.

Still, Cecil found many enjoyments in the ocean life. He loved watching the sun reflecting off the water, and the way the waves broke around the prow of the boat. Occasionally, dolphins would swim along with the ship, leaping out of the water, and Cecil had to be practically dragged away from the sight when he needed to return to work. He had not seen a whale yet, but he kept an eye out for one every moment he could.

He found that he liked the sailors as well. As cabin boy, he was the lowest ranking person on the ship, and so got all the jobs that no-one wanted to do, but the rest of the crew were friendly enough, joking with him and offering him smiles and encouragement. "He's a good lad," Cecil heard several times, when the sailors were discussing him, and he had to work hard to hide his smile.

Captain Rupert was less friendly with him on the sea than he had been in the cobbler's shop, but that made sense, Cecil knew, when Captain Rupert was no longer a family friend and truly his captain instead. But even so, Captain Rupert was a kind and fair master. He made Cecil work hard, but he seemed to appreciate Cecil's efforts, and as the days on the ocean passed, he found opportunities to let Cecil begin to learn a real sailor's work.

"Come here, lad!" he shouted, one calm day. "Johnny here'll teach you how to control the helm, eh?"

There was very little to actually control, as the weather was as peaceful as any Cecil had ever seen, and they were travelling in a straight line, but Cecil still felt a great thrill as he put his hands on the enormous wheel that controlled the ship for the first time. In quiet moments, when the risk of icebergs was low, Cecil was also allowed to take watch with several of the other men guiding him. Watch, he found, was far less enjoyable than the helm, as it involved a lot of standing and staring, and he had to maintain concentration even when there was absolutely nothing to see, but he did appreciate the quiet and the calm of it, after days running ragged up and down the ship completing his errands.

They first pulled into New York harbour ten days after the ship had departed from Bristol, and Cecil could not pull himself away from the sight of the strange buildings and streets as they approached. He had to stay aboard while all the passengers debarked, and then help with the unloading of all the cargo, but finally, finally, the sailors were allowed a little shore leave before the journey back to England.

Cecil had resolved to save as much money as he could, so he contented himself with wandering around the foreign city streets, but when Johnny the helmsman asked Cecil to lend him a little cash to get a few drinks, Cecil gladly obliged. He might never see the money again, but it made him even more popular amongst the crew, and although being known for generosity and kind-heartedness was not a good way to get rich, it was certainly a good way to make himself indispensable.

Cecil soon became familiar with the back and forth of the journey between New York and Bristol, and although the route meant that he could see his family and Samantha for at least a night or two every single month, he longed to travel even further afield. So, when about a year into Cecil's position as cabin boy, Captain Rupert announced that the ship would now be repurposed on a route between Bristol and Australia, stopping at the cape of South Africa along the way, Cecil was beyond excited. The journey was around 80 days each way, which meant a minimum of half a year away from his home and family at a time, but the rests in-between journeys were longer, and the crew would take every third journey off to remain at home.

Cecil's mother was less pleased about this development. She hugged him close with tears in her eyes, and begged him to be careful, while Jane declared that her brother simply must bring her back some strange Australian beasts as pets. The pay to sail to Australia was even better than the pay to New York, and his family no longer had to worry about rent with Cecil's extra income and one less mouth to feed. He even managed to begin saving a little money on top of the money he gave to his mother and uncle, and he dreamed of one day presenting it to Samantha and asking her to begin their life together.

Samantha, meanwhile, was heartbroken by the thought of Cecil's longer absences, having grown used to seeing him and hearing his stories at least once a month. But she put on a brave face for him, speculating about what exciting things he might see in that distant land and jokingly warning him to watch out for pirates along the way.

The years passed, and both Cecil and Samantha changed and grew. The once scrawny Cecil grew strong through hard work on the sea, and his skin developed a sun-kissed golden glow. Even his hair changed. It was still as messy as ever, but the Australian sun bleached it a paler brown.

Samantha grew into a beautiful young woman, and her large blue eyes and long golden curls attracted a lot of attention from potential suitors. The once shy flower seller had developed thick skin and a quick wit from years selling fish to men on the docks, and she handled any untoward comment with such a comment and a look as would immediately put any man back in his place.

Samantha's mother, Susan, was also aware of her daughter's growing beauty. The two of them still lived in a one-room house in the slums by the docks, and although they no longer went hungry, Susan had little hope that their fish-frying business would ever allow them to truly improve their situation.

But Samantha, she often thought, might be the answer. She was beautiful and hardworking, the two most desirable qualities in a wife, and Susan held out constant hope that one day a suitably rich suitor would appear for her daughter.

She was aware of Samantha's attachment to Cecil Fontaine, of course, but it did not concern her too much. Childhood romance rarely lasted, and the boy was away from Bristol for twelve months out of eighteen. A lot could change in twelve months, especially when a girl was only seventeen. She felt certain that their childish attachment would naturally die in short order, and Samantha would be open to the many more eligible suitors who might look her way.

It wasn't until Samantha was eighteen, however, that a truly promising suitor appeared. A handsome young man in well-made clothes began to stop by the fish stall every day, despite him looking far more well-to-do than their usual customers. He introduced himself as Trevor Collins, and Susan soon discovered that he was the son of the largest fishmonger in Bristol. This not only meant that he was rich, but also suggested he had highly specific reasons for visiting their food stall every day, for why would the son of a fishmonger need to purchase fried fish when he had so many fish available on his own doorstep?

"That Trevor Collins is a nice, handsome lad," Susan said casually one autumn evening, as the pair packed up their stall to head home.

Samantha made a non-committal noise of agreement.

"He likes you, you know," Susan said.

"I doubt it, Ma," Samantha said. "Why would he be interested in a girl like me? I'm sure he's got some rich girl back home he loves."

"No, you mark my words," Susan said. "A mother always knows these things."

Samantha just laughed. "Well," she said, "it's flattering if it's true, but I already have a fiancé, remember, Ma?"

"Who?" Susan asked. "That Cecil boy? You never told me you were engaged."

"We're not," Samantha said. "But we plan to be."

"Psh," Susan said. "When you get to my age, Samantha, and you've seen the things I've seen, you'll know not to count so much on the promises of a man, let alone a child like him! You've not seen him in near a year."

"But he's coming back," Samantha said. "He always promised he would, and I promised I'd wait for him."

"Is that really what you want?" Susan asked. "To never see your husband because he's always off having adventures at sea, while you're stuck at home trying to pay the rent and care for the babies? If you want my advice, Samantha, you'll forget all about that boy. You have a far better prospect right here in front of you."

CHAPTER SEVEN

Samantha had no intention of forgetting her promise to Cecil, and it stung that her mother could still be so dismissive of her love for a boy who, she often thought, had indirectly saved them both in their darkest time. Every time her mother attempted to offer some motherly wisdom, based on her lifetime of experience in the cruel world, Samantha's heart broke. It was as though her mother had no memory of the hardship Samantha had undergone after her father's death, when Susan had been unable to support them and Samantha had to fight for them both. Samantha did not dare to argue back, in case the memory upset her mother again, but it was difficult, she thought, to have gone through so much for one's mother and have none of it ever be appreciated.

Trevor Collins continued to visit the fish stall every day, and Samantha found herself analysing his every word and glance toward her, to see whether her mother might be correct regarding his feelings. It would be far easier if her mother was mistaken, because she could not imagine her mother letting go of the cause so easily if Trevor ever did actually propose.

She was disappointed to realise that her mother might not be entirely wrong. Trevor Collins smiled at her whenever he saw her, asking her about her day and her family in a way that was far friendlier than most customers. He always put the payment directly into her hand, and he allowed his skin to touch hers briefly every time. As much as she hated to admit it, having a fishmonger's son as such a loyal customer must mean either he hated his father and his family business, or he had a reason other than fish to visit Samantha every day.

"Samantha," he said one day. "I have a gift for you."

"A gift?" Samantha repeated, perplexed.

"Yes. Here." He pulled a small compact mirror out of his pocket and handed it to her. It was a fine thing, made from silver, with intricate metalwork in the pattern of a rose. It must have cost a week of Samantha's earnings, at the very least.

"Are you saying I have something on my face, Mr Collins?" she said with a casual smile. "That I need to check my reflection more often?"

"Well, you are truly beautiful, Samantha," he said. "It would be a shame if you could not see it for yourself."

Samantha felt herself blushing, but it was not with pleasure. She felt half embarrassed, half frustrated by his presumption. "Thank you, sir, but I have a mirror at home, and my mother would hate for me to become vain. One looking glass is enough for me."

"It's a gift," Mr Collins said, holding it out insistently towards her. "Surely you would not be rude enough to reject a gift?"

"Of course, she won't reject it," her mother said. She had been preparing fish about five paces away, but she hurried over now and took the small compact from Mr Collins' hand. "Samantha is such a shy girl. She does not know what to do when someone pays her attention."

"I cannot accept it," Samantha said again, but her mother shook her head.

"Nonsense, girl," she said. "Do not be rude to Mr Collins. You need not refuse on propriety's account. We all know Mr Collins is a good, upstanding young man."

Her mother put the mirror into her apron pocket.

"Thank the man for his generosity, Samantha," she said, and Samantha, still blushing, found she had no other alternative without seeming terribly rude.

"Thank you," she murmured, and Mr Collins smiled.

"Of course," he said. "A beautiful thing for a beautiful girl. Oh, is my fish ready?" he added, as Susan passed it to him. "Well, I had better be getting back to work before my father misses me. But I will see you soon, I hope, Miss Cole? And you, Mrs Cole."

"How could you be so rude?" Susan hissed at Samantha, after Trevor Collins had gone. "Have you no good sense at all?"

"I cannot accept a gift from him, Ma," Samantha said. "It isn't right. I can't entertain his pursuit. My heart belongs to another."

"I will not allow you to throw away such an opportunity," her mother said, "on such a foolish childhood promise. You will thank me, Samantha, when all is said and done. You will see."

But Samantha could not in good conscience keep the mirror, and neither could she return it. After agonising about what was best to do, she sold it at a pawnshop. The money would have been a great windfall for her and her mother, but it felt almost like stealing if she kept it for herself, so she distributed the earnings to the hungry around the docks.

A couple of days later, Mr Collins returned while Samantha's mother was away from the stall. "So, Samantha," he said. "Are you appreciating my gift?"

Something about his tone made Samantha's hackles rise. "No," she said. "I told you I could not in good conscience accept it."

Mr Collins continued to smile, but his eyes narrowed dangerously. "Then where is it?" he asked.

"Since you would not take it back, I sold it," Samantha said, sticking her chin up in defiance. "Don't worry. The money fed many people who otherwise might not have eaten that day."

"You sold it," Mr Collins said, in a low, steady voice, "and then you gave the money to beggars?"

"I gave the money to people who needed it," Samantha said, "far more than I did."

"It was not a gift for the beggars, Samantha. It was a gift for you. How can you expect the beggars to ever make anything of their lives if you hand out money to them?"

"How do you expect them to succeed," Samantha replied, "if they're starving to death?"

"If they are starving," Mr Collins said, "they should work for their bread. There is plenty of space at the workhouse, I'm sure."

Samantha stared at him in horror. What would Trevor Collins have made of her, ten years ago? Would he have thought that she deserved to starve, rather than be helped by Cecil and his family?

"It seems we must agree to disagree," she said. "Good day to you, Mr Collins."

Samantha expected that to be the end of it, but Trevor Collins returned to the stall on the next day, and the next. Each time, he complimented Samantha's beauty, and made snide comments about her overly sentimental heart, and Samantha found herself liking him less and less.

Then he brought her a second gift. "A necklace," he said, holding up the silver locket and chain, "to go around your pretty neck."

"Mr Collins," Samantha said again. "I cannot accept it."

"Don't be foolish, now, Miss Cole," he said. "Whatever reason could you have for not desiring such a pretty thing?"

"I am engaged, Mr Collins," she said firmly. "Therefore, I cannot accept any gift from you. It would not be right."

Mr Collins stared at her, his face turning red with anger. "You are engaged?"

"I am," she said, just as her mother rushed forward to interject.

"She is just being foolish, Mr Collins, as you said," her mother said. "She has a childish fancy for a sailor she knew in her youth. Nothing serious, and certainly no real engagement."

"Ma!" Samantha exclaimed, but her mother ignored her.

"I can only apologise, Mr Collins," her mother continued. "Do not hold her silliness against her."

"It is not silliness," Samantha insisted. "I am going to marry Cecil, Ma. I cannot accept any attention from Mr Collins or anybody else. I am certain Mr Collins understands me quite well."

"You are very clear," Mr Collins said. "If you value a poor sailor" he spat out the word like it was an insult "over me, then you are a fool indeed."

"Perhaps," Samantha said. "But a happy one."

Two weeks later, Samantha was standing at the docks when the Santa Lucia pulled into port. The grand ship was no longer as shiny and new as it had been when Cecil first climbed aboard, but its appearance was like an old friend to Samantha now. It meant Cecil, and Cecil meant home.

She watched the ship come to port, grinning from ear to ear, and waited patiently as first the ships passengers staggered off. Cecil had progressed from cabin boy by this point, but everyone had to help with the unloading of the ship, and so Samantha watched him from a distance as he first removed the passengers' stored luggage and then helped arrange the removal of the bigger freight.

Finally, finally, he was free. Samantha tried to content herself with waiting on the spot for him, with a little smile of pleasure, but as soon as her eyes met Cecil's, she knew she could not wait another moment for him. She raced across the space between them and threw her arms around him, and he wrapped his arms around her waist and picked her up in a spin as she laughed in delight.

"Sammie!" he said. "It's so good to see you."

"I can't believe you're home," Samantha said. "Seven months is too long."

"It is," Cecil said, "but I have gifts, if that helps."

Samantha immediately thought of Trevor Collins, and then hated herself, and him, for the intrusion on her joy. "Gifts?" she said. "The only gift I need is to see you."

"Well," Cecil said, "that and some shells I collected for you on the beach in southern Africa, and then again in Melbourne. I've had to carry them carefully all this way, so they didn't break."

"What?" Samantha asked. "No kangaroo?"

"The kangaroos!" Cecil cried. He grabbed her hand and spun her around again. "You will never guess what I saw this time. Tiny little kangaroos, only knee high."

"Babies?" Samantha asked.

"No, one of the men told me they were called wallabies. You would have loved them. They were just hopping their way through town like they owned the place."

"Good afternoon, there, Miss Cole," Captain Rupert said, coming up behind them. Samantha blushed slightly to be caught acting so giddily with Cecil, but she could not stop the grin spreading across her face.

"Good afternoon, sir," she said. "You returned my Cecil to me all in one piece?"

"Always have, and always will, miss," Captain Rupert said. "You can count on me for that. Now lad," he said, turning to Cecil. "I'm off to see that uncle of yours. He promised me new boots and a drink when we returned. But I'll tell him you got delayed doing some work on the ship. Give you a bit of extra time before your mother starts expecting you, eh?" And with a wink, he strode off across the docks.

CHAPTER EIGHT

Samantha always spent Cecil's first day back ashore deliriously happy. They walked around together, drinking coffee from a stand and peering at the brightly coloured goods in shop windows. Cecil bought them a bag of boiled sweets, for old time's sake, and they ate them while strolling through the city park, giggling like children over all the stories that each of them had missed.

Eventually, Samantha had to tell Cecil about Mr Collins, and her mother's encouragement of his suit. She tried to tell the story in an exaggerated, joking manner, so that Cecil would not take it too seriously or worry about him, but Cecil still frowned at the story's end, and took Samantha's hand in his.

"Sammie," he says. "Please promise me you'll be careful."

"You don't need to worry, Cecil," she said softly. "I care only for you."

"I never doubted that," Cecil said. "But I'm worried for you. What if he refuses to take no for an answer?"

"Oh, I don't think it's as serious as all that," Samantha said lightly. "And once we're married, it won't matter at all."

"That's true," Cecil said with a smile.

"When will that be, Cecil?" she asked, grabbing both of his hands in hers and turning to face him. "I can hardly bear the waiting any longer. My ma treats it like it's nothing. She's convinced that I'm going to forget you and choose someone else."

"How about this?" Cecil said. "Next time I come back to Bristol, I'll be staying for a few months. Let's get married then. We can do it as soon as I step off the ship, if you like."

"Right there on the docks?" she asked. "With all the seagulls watching?"

"The seagulls and the fishermen and all the people," he said. "And then I'll buy you a stick of rock for a wedding present, and we'll go ride at the funfair until we feel queasy."

"Sounds perfect," Samantha said. But then she frowned. "Does this mean you're leaving again soon? Is that why we have to wait?"

"I'm sorry, Sammie," Cecil said. "We got behind on this journey, with the bad weather, and we have to be careful with pirates about, so that can slow us even more. We'll be heading out again in just a week."

"Oh, Cecil," Samantha said, throwing her arms around him. She hugged him close, and he squeezed her tightly back. "You're never home for long enough." She stepped back. "But next time you come home, we'll be married, won't we?"

"I promise you, Samantha. The next time I step off a ship onto Bristol docks, the only thing I will be thinking about is marrying you."

Samantha smiled and pulled him in to press a sweet kiss to his lips.

"Now tell me about these pirates," she said.

Samantha spent the evening with Cecil's family, eating dinner and listening to their jokes and stories. She tried to visit Cecil's mother and sisters whenever she could, partly to make sure they were all right without Cecil, partly to feel closer to him, and partly because she truly loved their company. Still, it had been a couple of weeks since she had last sat down for dinner with them, and the girls were full of stories of school and mischief.

"We have something to tell you," Cecil said to his mother and Uncle Acker, after dinner was finished.

"You eloped!" his sister Mary shouted.

"You got Captain Rupert to marry you on the ship!" Anna exclaimed.

"You're running off to become a pirate!" Jane suggested.

Cecil and Samantha laughed. "No, no, and only if the treasure is particularly good," Cecil said. "But I've asked Samantha to marry me, and she's said yes."

If he expected a big, sentimental reaction, he didn't get it. Jane rolled her eyes, and Anne picked up half a roll of bread to lob at him, shouting, "That's not news!" Even his mother only smiled fondly at them both, and said, "That's wonderful, dears," without any real surprise in her voice whatsoever.

"Well, I thought it was exciting," Cecil grumbled.

"Lad, we've known you two were going to get married since you were ten years old," Uncle Acker said. "And you've both talked like it was guaranteed to happen since you were thirteen. If you only proposed today, I don't know what took you so long."

"It isn't that," Samantha said with a smile. "We've known for a while. But now he's nearly twenty, and moving up in the ranks, and since he's going to be home for a few months next time he is here, we decided we wish to get married when he returns from this next voyage. So hopefully only six months from now. Seven, if we're really unlucky."

"And we'll be so happy to have you," Cecil's mother said, pulling Samantha into a hug and kissing her on the cheek. "Though it will hardly feel different. You've been a part of this family for so long. I suppose now it will just finally be official."

Uncle Acker clapped Cecil on the back, grinning, and headed to the cupboard to find something celebratory to drink. Meanwhile, Samantha was embraced by all three of Cecil's younger sisters, with Mary immediately launching into questions about what sort of dress she planned to wear and how she would style her hair.

Despite her sadness that Cecil would soon be gone again, Samantha returned home positively skipping with joy. But once she entered the one-room house she shared with her mother, she remembered she still had one potentially unpleasant chore to complete.

She had to tell her mother.

"You could do so much better," her mother exclaimed, when she heard the news. "A sailor, and not even a high-ranking one."

"He'll be high-ranking one day," Samantha said. "He's not even twenty. And even if he isn't, I don't care about that, Ma. I love him."

"Love!" Her mother shook her head. "You'll see how far love gets you when you need money to put food on the table."

"Ma," Samantha said. "Why are you so against Cecil? He has never been anything but kind and generous to either of us."

Samantha's mother took her hands in hers. "I married your father for love," she said. "When we were very young. He didn't have much money, but I didn't care, because I thought love was enough. And when he died, I was left with nothing except a broken heart. I married a man who I loved and who loved me, and that did not stop him from dying and leaving me to face the world alone. Money would have got me farther in life, Samantha, than love ever did."

Samantha slid her hands out of her mother's. "Are you saying you regret marrying papa?" she asked.

"I regret losing your papa," her mother said. "I don't know what my life would even be if I had not married him. But Sammie, I've been down the path where you think love is enough. What will happen to you if you lose Cecil? Or if he changes, grows bored with you, or becomes cruel? What will happen if you grow sick and he is not here to care for you? What happens if the money is not enough for rent, and he sails off on a ship, leaving you and your children to struggle alone?"

"That isn't who Cecil is, Mama. He wouldn't do that."

"No one can truly know the future, Sammie," she said. She sighed. "If you truly wish to marry the boy, then you do not exactly have my blessing, but I will not stand in your way. But please, Samantha. Think carefully."

"I have, Mama," Samantha said. "Believe me. I have been thinking about it my whole life, and I know my heart. I could not be happy with anyone else."

The Santa Lucia sailed out of Bristol a week later, and Samantha stood on the docks to watch it leave, waving at the ship with the crowd despite knowing that Cecil must be too busy working to see her. It was always heart breaking to see the ship sail away, but Samantha felt great hope too. Next time she saw that ship, she knew, she and Cecil would finally get married, and their future could truly begin.

CHAPTER NINE

Samantha did not hear word about the Santa Lucia for many months, but that was not unusual. Cecil sent her a letter with another boat travelling back to England when the ship docked for a couple of days on the cape of Africa, but once the Santa Lucia had passed that great continent, there was really no way to send messages any quicker than simply carrying them in the ship and passing them personally when they returned.

Because of that, Samantha was not concerned when she did not hear a single word about Cecil or the Santa Lucia for several months. Six months passed since the Santa Lucia's departure from Bristol, and she began to listen for news of the ship being sighted coming around Plymouth, but when she did not hear any reports, she was not overly concerned. The journey to Australia was a long one, and any number of things could delay the journey. Six months away was always the optimistic hope, but it was often seven.

Still, seven months passed, and there was no word of the ship. Samantha began to enquire at the docks every day, but no one had any news. She began to worry that something terrible had happened. Had they been delayed or damaged by a storm? Had the steam engines broken, forcing them to rely on sails alone?

Eight months after Samantha saw the Santa Lucia sail out of Bristol, she headed down to the docks to find a sombre note in the air. She passed a woman weeping by the railings, and the normal clatter and clamour of work had a decidedly subdued tone. Samantha's stomach dropped, but she told herself that she was being silly. Anything might have happened, involving any boat.

She marched to the harbourmaster's office, and paled when she saw his ashen face. "What has happened?" she asked him. "Is it—"

"I am so very sorry, miss," the harbourmaster said, in a low sincere voice. "News arrived of the Santa Lucia this morning."

"And?" Samantha asked.

"The ship was set upon by pirates, miss," he said. "They don't usually target large liners like that, but they did. I am afraid that everyone aboard is presumed dead."

Samantha swayed on her feet. "Presumed dead?" she asked. "It is not known?"

"I am sorry, miss," the harbourmaster said. "The crew may never be found, or the ship itself, but we feel quite certain of the attack. It happened within sight of the shore, and it was witnessed, although from a distance, so there are no details."

"But," Samantha said, "at such a distance, how could anyone know which ship was involved? It could have been any liner."

"I am sorry," the harbourmaster said again. "There are few liners of that size travelling in those waters, and the Santa Lucia was the only one at the time. It is quite certain that it was the victim of an attack, and as no news has reached us of a single crewmember or passenger since that time, they are all lost, miss."

It could not be true. Samantha's legs gave out from under her, and she collapsed to the ground. "Miss!" the harbourmaster said. "Miss!" But Samantha could not reply. She stared at the wooden planks beneath her, her vision blurring. Cecil could not be lost. Not him, not his crewmates, not Captain Rupert. It could not be true. They were meant to be getting married. How could he not return, when he had promised he would?

Tears ran down her cheeks as she shook her head, over and over again. She could not believe it. She would not believe it.

But she already knew in her heart the reality of the harbourmaster's words. The ship had been delayed for too long to deny it.

Cecil was not coming back.

~

The harbourmaster's wife was called to the docks to help Samantha to her feet, and she was kind enough to help Samantha home. Samantha lay down in her bed, staring at the wall, until her mother came looking for her mid-afternoon, worried that her daughter had not returned to the fish stall to work.

"My poor, dear girl," her mama said, brushing a hand soothingly through Samantha's hair as she sobbed. "This is what I feared for you, my love. Hush, now. It will be alright."

Samantha did not rise from her bed for two days. But slowly, she came back to herself, and all at once she remembered May Fontaine, and Uncle Acker, and all of Cecil's sisters who must by now have heard the news. She leapt up at once, and, hardly pausing to even grab a shawl against the cold, raced from the cottage.

Cecil's family had heard the news. The story had even appeared in the newspaper that morning, and when Samantha arrived at their apartment, she found Uncle

Acker sitting with the paper in front of him, reading it over and over, as though it might help him understand.

Cecil's mother pulled Samantha into an immediate hug, and the two women cried together. "I am so sorry," Samantha sobbed to May. "I am so, so sorry."

Cecil's mother just held her tighter.

There was no body to bury, so the family held a simple ceremony by the water, all of them dressed in black. After the funeral, Samantha returned to work at the fish stall, she and her mother could little afford to eat without her, but she continued to dress in her mourning black, and she felt as though all the joy and colour had been leeched out of the world.

Her heart could not entirely give up its hope that she would see Cecil again, that there must have been some mistake, some misunderstanding, and he was travelling his way back to her and his family even now. But the months passed, and no further news came. If Cecil was alive, surely he would have sent a message somehow to reassure them all. He would have found a way.

Samantha spent all the time she could with Cecil's mother and sisters. Her grief was more bearable, she found, when she could share it with others, and although she knew that her own mother was well-meaning, she could not forget her bias against Cecil while he was alive. In the Fontaine's kitchen, she could listen to his mother's fond remembrances by the fire, or just sit in the quiet while his mother sewed, knowing that he was treasured in both their hearts.

Trevor Collins continued to visit the fish stall on most days, but he brought no further gifts, and Samantha was too weighed down by grief to spend much time or attention considering his presence. He was always polite, and Samantha's mother often gave him more fried fish than he had technically paid for, but he seemed to have taken Samantha's previous declarations about Cecil to heart, and he did not pressure her again. Indeed, he had expressed his most sincere sounding condolences for Samantha's loss soon after the story of the Santa Lucia appeared in the newspapers.

It felt to Samantha that all time should have stopped with Cecil's death, but it marched on. Winter turned to spring, and then to summer, and as the autumn leaves began to fall from the trees, Samantha found that although her grief for Cecil was no less, she was able to manage it more. For the first few months, it had been a shadow that smothered everything, gripping tightly around her lungs and making it almost impossible to breathe. A year on, it was more like a shadow that travelled along beside her. Sometimes it attempted to smother her again, but most of the time, it was a companion at her side, almost comforting in its familiarity.

But one thing that did not change was Samantha's official mourning. She had never been able to afford all new clothes in the heavy, formal black crepe or bombazine that the middle class ladies wore to mourn their loves in Bristol, but she had dyed all her existing dresses black. Even though a year was generally considered more than adequate time to begin shifting to slightly lighter shades, like grey or lilac, that, to Samantha, felt like beginning to let go of Cecil, and she did not think she would ever be ready for that day.

Her mother, however, disagreed. A year after the disappearance of the Santa Lucia, Samantha's mother stopped her as she prepared to step out of the house to work one morning. "My dear," she said. "I must talk to you. You have been in mourning for over a year. Even a widow would be in half mourning by now, and you were only engaged. Do you not think it is time to move on?"

"The queen has been in full mourning for her husband for over fifteen years," Samantha said.

"She is the queen, Samantha," her mother said. "She can do as she wishes. And again, she is widowed. You are not."

"It would feel wrong," Samantha confessed, "to dress differently or to move on. I still miss him as on the first day I learned of his death."

"But my dear," her mother said, "you cannot grieve forever. One day you must find a new husband, and no one will think to consider you while you are dressed as you are."

Samantha shook her head. "I will never marry another man," she said. "Cecil was destined to be my husband. We were meant to be together. God may have taken him from me before I had that chance, but I want no one else. I will wait for him until we can be reunited again."

"Samantha, really," her mother said. "You should not speak like this. You must marry someone. You cannot pledge your soul to a ghost."

"He is not a ghost, Mama," Samantha said. "He is Cecil. I have quite made up my mind. Please, do not mention it again."

CHAPTER TEN

Christmas was almost upon them when Trevor Collins approached the fish stall one chilly, grey afternoon, a brown paper bag in his hands. When Samantha saw the packet, she was immediately reminded of Cecil carrying boiled sweets just for her, and a smile formed at the memory.

"Miss Cole," Mr Collins said, as he strode up to the stall. "Good afternoon."

"Good afternoon, Mr Collins," she said.

"You seem well, Miss Cole, if you don't mind my saying so."

"Thank you, Mr Collins," she said. "I was remembering something very dear to me. I think it did me good."

"Your smiling face is certainly a balm for a cold winter day," he said. "I hope I can see it more often. I have brought you a gift."

He held out the brown paper bag, but Samantha shook her head. "Mr Collins," she said, "I couldn't possibly-"

"They're hot roasted chestnuts," he said, "for you and your mother. I thought it must be cold, working out here by the docks, so when I stopped by the stall to get some for myself, I thought I would get some for you as well, to say thank you for all the delicious lunches you've given me."

"Well," Samantha said, "alright. Thank you." She took the bag from him. The heat of the chestnuts inside immediately warmed her hands. "That is very kind of you."

"It's a pleasure, Miss Cole," he said, with a tip of his hat.

A few days later, it was Christmas Eve, and a light mist had fallen over the city. Samantha's mother had returned to their home at lunchtime with a bad head cold, so Samantha was running the stall alone, but she found she liked the quiet of it. The lamplighters were out, and the lights cast a hazy glow across the streets through the mist.

Samantha pulled her shawl a little tighter around her shoulders and thought of the day to come tomorrow. For once, she and her mother had been able to take the whole of Christmas Day off, and Samantha had been saving for their meal for the entire year. She had even been able to buy a small goose, and Cecil's mother had given her a beautiful looking plum pudding for the two of them to share. Samantha was looking forward to the rare treat, and, if it did not rain too harshly, she hoped to take a walk along the harbour, before visiting the stone that had been laid down in Cecil's memory.

She was so lost in her thoughts that she did not notice Trevor Collins approaching the stall. "Merry Christmas to you, Miss Cole," he shouted to her, and she jumped, but then smiled.

"Merry Christmas to you too, Mr Collins," she said. "Has your father closed up for the season, then?"

"Not yet, Miss Cole," he said. "He'll work us 'til the last moment he possibly can. But I managed to slip out for a moment. I was afraid you would be retiring with the sun, and then I would not be able to give you this." He pulled a small parcel from his pocket, wrapped in brown paper and tied with string. "It is a Christmas present for you, Miss Cole."

"Oh," Samantha said, blushing. "I couldn't possibly;"

"Have you not heard, Miss Cole? It is terribly bad luck to refuse a Christmas present. Why, you will have bad luck for all of the year to come. And it is just a small gift, to show my appreciation. Please. Take it."

"But I don't have anything for you," she said.

"Since when is a lady expected to give a gift to a gentleman?" he said. "Please. Allow me to thank you." He placed the package down on the table in front of her. "Until next time, Miss Cole."

"Goodbye, Mr Collins," she whispered, and with a bow, he strode away into the mist.

She picked up the parcel and weighed it in her hands. It was fairly light. Perhaps it would be no great harm for her to open it, she thought. It might well just be sweets or a small favour of familiar appreciation from his mother to hers.

She carefully unwrapped it and then opened the box inside. A brooch sat nestled in crinkled paper, bearing the design of a dove. It was black and silver, perfectly acceptable suitable jewellery for a woman entering half-mourning, but the meaning behind that seemed clear. It was a transition piece, for a woman moving on from loss, and for her to be given it by another gentleman, who had expressed interest in her before, was inappropriate in her mind.

It was too late to return it to him that night. He had vanished into the mist, and Samantha could not leave the stall alone to chase him. She was forced to slide the box into her pocket, and she resolved to return the expensive gift the very next time she saw him.

Finally, she sold the last of their fish for the day, and retired home to her mother.

The feast the following day was a delicious one, and although Samantha and her mother still had little money to spare, they managed to sit down by the fire and exchange a few small gifts after it was over. Samantha had managed to find a simple but elegant pendant for her mother, along with a new comb she had found second-hand but in excellent condition.

Samantha's mother gave her two new dresses, one for every day, and one for Sunday best, in delicate lilac.

"Ma—" Samantha begin, when she saw the contents of the package, but her mother cut her off before she could argue.

"Now listen to me," she said. "You cannot wear black for the rest of your life, Samantha. You must move on one day. Transitioning to lilac does not mean that you have forgotten your Cecil or moved on from him. Half mourning means that you carry your grief with you, instead of being overwhelmed with it. Is that not as you told me you felt, a few weeks ago? It is time, my dear."

"But his family—" Samantha said.

"His mother and uncle gave me some of the money for the dresses," her mother said. "They do not want you wrapped up in black for the rest of your life for Cecil's sake either, dear. And neither would Cecil. A new year, my dear, and a new step."

"But I cannot," Samantha said. "If I do, it will look like I am signalling that I am ready to consider love again, and after Trevor Collins' gift to me, he will read more into it than he should."

"Trevor Collins gave you a Christmas gift?" her mother asked.

"Yes," Samantha said. "I must have forgotten to mention it." She put her hand into her pocket and pulled out the box. "He gave me this."

Her mother took the box from her. Her eyes widened when she opened it and saw the brooch.

"This is quite a gift, Sammie," she said.

"I cannot accept it," Samantha said. "I must return it to him when I see him next. I didn't realise what it was."

"You must do no such thing, Sammie!" her mother said. "You cannot reject such a rich and generous gift."

"I must, Mama," Samantha said, "precisely because it's so rich and generous. It has meaning and implications that I can't possibly accept."

"And why not?" her mother asked. "It is not yet an engagement. And he is a dependable, kind man."

"I have told you why not, Mama," Samantha said. "I never intend to marry, now that Cecil is gone."

"Don't be foolish, child," her mother said. "Look where we live. Look at the Christmas we had to scrape all year to put together. Trevor Collins' family would have eaten a goose three times the size of ours, and the cost would never have even been a thought to them. They probably have a housekeeper to worry about such things. A connection with that boy would change our fortunes for good."

"But I cannot, Mama," Samantha said.

"You are still young, Samantha," her mother said, "but you won't remain that way forever. If you reject your suitors now, in ten years you will find yourself desperately wishing for a single one even a tenth as good as Trevor Collins. You will get older, and you will realise that this world is not kind to a woman who is alone, regardless of what noble reason she thinks she has for refusing to marry. You will be lonely, and hungry, and tired for all your endless work, and you will look back on this and wish you had taken Trevor Collins more seriously. And you may be happy to risk that regret, but I will not allow it. It is my job as your mother to ensure your happiness, and I cannot allow you to destroy it in this way. You will keep the brooch, Samantha, and be thankful for it."

CHAPTER ELEVEN

The following day, Samantha rose early, dressed in her familiar black, and slipped out of the door before her mother awoke. With the brooch safe in its box in her pocket, she walked along the harbour in the pre-dawn light, waiting until she could be reasonably certain that Trevor Collins' fishmongers would be open.

It was a sizeable shop, with many boxes of fish arranged with signs and prices under a canopy out front. Several women were already picking their way through the choices for the day, and Samantha walked past them into the shop itself.

A plump middle-aged woman with a face remarkably similar to Trevor Collins' smiled at her as she entered.

"Can I help you, dear?" she asked.

"Yes," Samantha said. "I was wondering if Mr Trevor Collins was available."

"And who might be asking, dear?"

"My name is Samantha Cole," she said. "I'm a friend."

Trevor's mother's smile grew far wider as recognition sparked in her eyes. "Ah," she said. "Trevor's famous sweetheart. Yes, of course, of course, come in. He's just back there. He'll be delighted to see you." She gestured to a door just to the right of the counter.

Samantha wanted to correct her about the nature of their relationship, but the woman looked so happy that she found it difficult to crush that. Instead, she nodded and followed the woman's directions into the rear of the shop.

She located Trevor Collins at once, just from his voice. "Were you born this much of a fool," he was shouting, "or did you get hit on the head as a baby? I asked for more mackerel, not more cod, you great oaf."

"They didn't have any more mackerel," another, younger-sounding voice said. "They only had the cod."

"And you took them at their word? Why do I have to work with such idiots?" Samantha heard a crash, like a hand slamming down on a table. "Take it back. Fix it. Or don't ever think of coming back here again."

"Of course, sir," the voice said. "At once, sir."

Samantha waited a moment for the employee's footsteps to fade away, and then walked around the corner.

"Miss Cole!" he said, his tone suddenly all kindness and civility. "What a delightful surprise."

"What if he was telling the truth?" she asked softly. "What if there really was no mackerel to be had?"

"What?" he asked. "Oh, the boy before. Don't worry about him. He's so much of a fool, I'm surprised he managed to bring back fish at all. He'd probably buy duck for us if the suppliers sold it. A little fear will do him good."

"Do you often try to give your employees a little fear?" she asked.

"When it's needed," he said. "My father didn't become the biggest fishmonger in Bristol from kindness. But what can I do for you?"

Samantha's nerve was slightly shaken from hearing Mr Collins shout, but, she told herself, that was no excuse not to do what was right. If Mr Collins had a fearful temper, then she had all the more reason to refuse his pursuit.

"I came," she said, "to thank you for my Christmas gift, and to tell you that I unfortunately cannot accept it."

"Cannot accept it?" Mr Collins asked, with a laugh. "You already did."

"That was before I realised what it was," she said. "It is too large a gift."

"Oh, is that all?" Mr Collins asked. "You are too modest, Miss Cole. I assure you that such a trifle is hardly generous enough a gift for a woman of your grace and beauty."

"I mean," Samantha said, holding the box out, "that I hope I am not being presumptuous in thinking it the sort of gift a suitor might give his betrothed, and if that is the case, then I cannot in good conscious keep it. Perhaps my mother has not told you, but I am still in mourning for my lost fiancé, and I do not believe I will ever marry now. I cannot accept it."

Mr Collins made no move to take the box. "You are not being presumptuous," he said, "in making that assumption. I think I've made my feelings about you quite clear, Miss Cole. I had patience, while you were still mooning over that boy, and I have given you a great deal of time to recover from the shock of his death. But your mother tells me you will be coming out of mourning soon, and I wanted to make certain that no one beat me to the chase in pursuing you."

"There is no chase," Samantha said. "I am not leaving mourning. Please believe me when I tell you that I do not intend to get married to anybody. I cannot accept your gift."

"It is already yours," Mr Collins said. "My own mother helped me to select it."

"And I'm grateful," Samantha said. "But truly—"

"You are not listening to me, Miss Cole," he said, his words louder and harsher now. "It is yours. I wish for you to have it. I have given you ample time to recover from your imagined loss, but the time for that is over."

"Imagined loss?" Samantha cried, but Mr Collins was not finished.

"I have been beyond patient," he said, "but I made my intentions clear to you two years ago, and my patience is growing thin. I intend to marry you, Miss Cole. Your mother certainly approves of the match, and I can promise you that you will not find a better suitor than me."

Samantha stared at him, bristling with fury, but what could she say in response to such a declaration? He seemed determined to ignore every word she spoke.

"I am quite alright with that, Mr Collins," she said. "Good day to you." And placing the box on the table, she strode from the room.

The next morning, Samantha was getting ready for the day when she noticed that her usual day dress was missing. She searched for it about the cottage, but when she opened the chest where she kept her clothes, she found that all of her black dresses were missing. Only the lilac remained, along with a couple of grey dresses that Samantha had never seen before.

"Mama," Samantha said, her stomach sinking with dread. "Where are my dresses?"

"I went out early this morning and gave them away, dear," her mother replied. "Young Mrs Smith just went into mourning for her husband, and she had nothing to wear. Well, I told her you were going into half-mourning and no longer needed your black, so we agreed to exchange some of your mourning wardrobe for a couple of grey dresses that she owned."

Samantha's hands shook with anger, but she forced herself to close her eyes and take a calming breath before she spoke. "Mama," she said. "I told you that I did not want to leave full mourning."

"And I told you that I would not allow your foolishness to put your future happiness and security at risk. It ends now, Samantha. Now get dressed, quickly, or we will be late."

Unless Samantha wished to head out in her nightgown, she had no choice but to change into the lilac dress. As she was buttoning it up the back, she saw something else that shocked her. Trevor Collins' brooch was pinned just below the right shoulder.

"Mama," she said slowly. "Where did you get this?"

"Oh, I saw Mr Collins yesterday afternoon," she said. "He said you visited his shop to thank him for the gift and then forgot to take it with you. I thought it would look very nice on your new dress, so I pinned it there."

"I returned it to Mr Collins, Mama," Samantha said. She finished buttoning up her dress and then moved to unpin the brooch. It would not come undone. Her mother had applied some trick with thread, she saw, to make it almost impossible to detach the brooch while the dress was being worn, at least without risking tearing the dress itself in the process. "Mama!" she cried.

"No, Samantha," she said. "I will not hear another word about it. You are lucky that Mr Collins has not abandoned his suit entirely. He must love you far more than you possibly deserve. Now we are running late. You will wear the lilac, and you will wear the brooch, and if we are lucky enough to see him again today, you will thank him for his kindness and ask his forgiveness for your rudeness. Do I make myself clear, Samantha?"

"Yes, Mama," Samantha said. "Perfectly clear."

CHAPTER TWELVE

T revor Collin appeared as expected at lunchtime. His eyes fell approvingly on Samantha's lilac dress and the brooch pinned to her shoulder, and Samantha felt sick. She wanted to shout that this had not been her choice, that her mother had forced her into it, but her mother was standing close beside her, a warning hand on her arm, and she remained silent.

"Mrs Cole," Mr Collins said cheerful. "It's good to see you here again. You were missed on Christmas Eve."

"Thank you, Mr Collins," Samantha's mother said.

"You are recovered from your chill, I hope?"

"Yes, yes, quite recovered," she said. "Although it is difficult, you know. The drafts are truly terrible on one's health. I am often more ill than I should be, I fear."

"I am sorry to hear that," Mr Collins said. "I hope one day soon, perhaps, you will have somewhere warmer to live."

"That would be wonderful, Mr Collins," Samantha's mother said. "I hope that will be the case."

"Would you mind if I borrowed Miss Cole for a stroll?" he asked. "I promise to return her to you promptly."

"I have to work," Samantha said quickly, but her mother laughed.

"Take as long as you like," she said. Mr Collins held out the crook of his arm to Samantha. Samantha ignored it, but she did reluctantly step around the stall to stand beside him and allow him to lead her along the harbour.

"Miss Cole," he said, once they were out of earshot of her mother. "I am so glad to see that you've reconsidered after our conversation yesterday."

Samantha shook her head. "I have not, Mr Collins. My mother supports your suit, and she told me to wear this today, but I'm very much still in mourning, and I have no intention of ever marrying anybody."

"Miss Cole," he said. Then, "Samantha. I understand that you are shy, but you must stop fighting the inevitable. Our parents approve. We are well matched for one another. I can give you and your mother a life far beyond what you currently have. Why are you resisting this?"

"Because I don't love you," Samantha said sharply, and then flinched at the harshness of her words, but Trevor Collins barely even seemed to react.

"You will," he said. "In time." He seemed thoughtful for a moment. "What is it you want, Samantha? What are you holding out for?"

"I am not holding out for anything," Samantha insisted, but he cut her off.

"Is it a new home for your mother? She cannot live with us, but if you want somewhere warmer and safer for her to live, that can be arranged."

Samantha opened her mouth to protest again, but the words would not come out. Her mother had not been lying before, when she said the drafts in their tiny cottage had affected her health. Her mother was more unwell than she should be, and she only coughed more as the years passed. Could she really reject an offer that would improve her mama's health, even if it came from such a man?

"I see I have persuaded you," Mr Collins said. "Consider it done."

"No," Samantha said. "I couldn't possibly-"

"Consider it a wedding present," Mr Collins said.

Samantha felt as though she might cry. The loss of Cecil still affected everything, and her heart ached every day for his return. Even if she were ready to marry, even if she thought she might ever be, she would not choose Trevor Collins for herself. His temper and his forceful attitude made her uneasy, but he was penning her in, bit by bit, and with her mother supporting his pursuit, she was beginning to feel as though she could not breathe.

"Samantha," he said. "Do you accept?"

"Was that intended as a proposal?" Samantha asked, taken aback.

"If you accept it."

"No," Samantha said. "I cannot accept it. Please, Mr Collins. If you'll excuse me-"

She tried to step away, but Trevor Collins seized her arm. His fingers pressed into the skin below her elbow, hard enough to bruise, and when Samantha gasped in pain and tried to pull herself free, he refused to let go.

"Now you listen here, Samantha," he said, in a low, dangerous voice. "I am growing tired of your games. We will be wed, you and I. I recommend you do not waste the opportunity you have, or things will go poorly for you."

"Let go of me," Samantha gasped. "You're hurting me."

He released her arm, and she stumbled back.

"Think on what I've said, Samantha," he said, and with a nod of his head, he strode away.

Trevor Collins was as good as his word. Barely a week later, his father appeared at the fish stall to meet Samantha's mother, and told her all about the cottage he owned in a nicer part of town that was currently going to be unoccupied, not far from Trevor's own home. It would be the perfect home, he commented, for the mother of Trevor's bride, so that they would not need to be separated long, and although Samantha's mother only smiled and said what a kind-hearted thought that was, she understood the man's meaning perfectly.

"A cottage," she hissed to Samantha later. "Cecil Fontaine could not have offered that. A better opportunity will not come along, Sammie. When he proposes, you must accept."

Samantha felt more and more walled in on all sides. She was trapped, and she did not know how she might possibly escape. The next day, she pled a headache from her mother to avoid heading to the stall, and since Samantha never normally missed a day of work for anything, her mother reluctantly left her to rest.

It was not entirely a lie. Samantha's head ached fiercely, and her heart thudded so insistently in her chest that it was growing difficult for her to breathe. Still, Samantha only waited ten minutes after her mother's departure before heading out herself.

Uncle Acker's cobbler's shop had hardly changed in the twelve years that Samantha had known him. When Samantha opened the door, the bell above it rang with the same insistent cheeriness that she had heard the very first time she stepped inside. The stools for customers were a little more worn, and Uncle Acker had more grey in his hair and beard, but it was still the same, familiar place.

Uncle Acker looked up from his work when the bell rang and smiled. "Miss Cole," he said. "It's always a pleasure to see you."

"You as well, Uncle," she said. "Is Mrs Fontaine available?"

"Yes, yes, she's upstairs doing some sewing," Uncle Acker said. "Head on up."

"Thank you," Samantha murmured, and Uncle Acker frowned.

"Is everything all right, lass?" he asked. "You look troubled, if you don't mind my saying so."

"I am troubled," Samantha admitted.

"Then you had better speak to May," he said. "She always knows what to do in a pinch."

Samantha smiled at him and nodded.

Upstairs, Cecil's mother was working at the kitchen table, mending the seam on a pair of men's trousers. She smiled when she saw Samantha, and she rose to envelop her in a hug.

"My dear," she said warmly. "It is good to see you."

Samantha could not help it. She burst into tears.

"Oh, dear," May Fontaine said. "Whatever is the matter? Whatever it is, I am certain we can set it right. Hush now, dear. Come sit and tell me."

Samantha took a seat beside her at the kitchen table and launched into the tale. She told Mrs Fontaine about Trevor Collins' pursuit, and the way her mother was pushing her to accept the match. She told her about her doubts and fears about his character, and how, even if he were the sweetest man in the world, she did not want to marry anybody and leave Cecil behind. Tears ran down her cheeks as she spoke.

"What am I to do, Mrs Fontaine?" she said. "My mother is insisting I marry him, and I don't know how I can refuse him, when he's offering us so much good. If I turn him down, I'm abandoning my mother to suffer, when she has the chance to live a better life. But I can't abandon Cecil. I can't."

Cecil's mother rubbed a soothing hand across Samantha's back. "As far as I see it," she said, "there are two problems here. I don't think you should marry anybody who you think will make you unhappy. It is unfair for your mother to put so much responsibility on your shoulders. If you don't want to marry him, my dear, then you shouldn't marry him. But don't make that decision for Cecil's sake. I love my son very much, and I know you have loved him too. But as much as it breaks my heart to admit it, he is gone, Samantha, and he is never coming back. He would never have expected you to remain unmarried your whole life in his memory. He would have wanted you to be happy, Samantha. He would have wanted you to find love again. So please, don't shut yourself away from the world for his sake."

Samantha wiped the tears from her eyes and nodded. "It's just hard," she said, "to accept that he's truly gone. Sometimes I still think he might appear on the horizon, sailing into the harbour, if I just believe in him enough. How can I believe he will never come home?"

"I feel the same," May said. "But Cecil loved you very much. If there were a way for him to get home, or a way for him to contact you, he would have found it. You cannot wait for him your whole life, Sammie. Someday, you will need to let go."

CHAPTER THIRTEEN

"**T**revor Collins came by the stall again today," Samantha's mother said that night, as they settled down for supper. "He asked after you."

Samantha nodded. She could not think of any response to the statement that would satisfy her mother, so she said nothing. Both her thoughts and her heart were still churning from her conversation with Cecil's mother.

"He was very sorry to hear you were unwell," her mother continued. "You will have to come in tomorrow, so he can see you are alright."

"Yes, Mama," Samantha murmured.

"I told him," her mother continued, "that grief had made you foolish, but you were finally ready to see sense. I am certain he is going to propose soon, Sammie, and you must accept him."

"Mama—" Samantha began, but her mother spoke over her.

"No, Sammie," she said. "You will not waste this chance. So, let me tell you this. You may marry Trevor Collins or not, as you please. But if you don't marry him, you can't stay here, and you can't work at the fish stall any longer either. If you're so insistent that you can make your own way in the world, then you may do so, but don't do it here."

Samantha gaped at her mother in horror. Samantha had been the one to find this home when they could no longer afford rent on their old flat after her father died. Samantha had been the one with the idea to fry and sell fish. She had worked so hard to support herself and her mother, from such a young age. Her mother could not take that away from her.

But she saw in her mother's face that she was determined. No arguments would dissuade her.

When Trevor Collins arrived at the stall again the following evening and asked for a walk with Samantha, she forced herself to smile and agree. She took his arm as they walked along the harbour, and Samantha's heart was soothed somewhat by the sound of the waves on the air. She felt as though Cecil were with her, watching over her. But Cecil could not protect her from her current situation.

"Your mother," Trevor Collins began, "has led me to believe you have had a change of heart, Samantha. Please tell me, and make me the happiest man in all of Bristol. Marry me, Samantha, and be my wife."

A lump rose in Samantha's throat, making it difficult to speak. "I am still in half-mourning," she said slowly. "If I cast it off too quickly and marry you, people will think poorly of us both. Our marriage will be cursed by my lack of proper duty. I would rather wait, and have an auspicious future, than rush and ruin it all."

"What are you saying, Samantha?"

"Yes," she said, hating herself for the words. "I will marry you. But I cannot yet. We must wait a year and a day. After that, then, yes. I will be your bride."

Trevor Collins grinned. "I am loath to wait even a moment longer," he said, "but you are right. A little wait will do no harm. A year and a day, Samantha." He took her hand in his and pressed it to his lips. Samantha shivered, instantly filled with fear and regret. She had only delayed her problem, not cured herself of it entirely. But perhaps, in the year, she would get a chance to breathe. Perhaps she would figure out a solution.

Then Trevor Collins was leaning down to kiss her. Samantha blushed and stepped away. "We are in public," she said softly. "And I am in mourning. It would be improper."

Trevor frowned, and then nodded. "You are right, my love," he said. "We must wait. But soon, we will be together always."

Samantha could not force herself to smile, but if Trevor noticed, he did not seem to care.

Reactions to the engagement were exactly as Samantha would have imagined them to be. Her mother was delighted, embracing her daughter and her future son-in-law, her smile full of triumph. Trevor's mother said she was delighted to have such a beautiful daughter-in-law, and she invited Samantha and her mother to dine with them as soon as they possibly could.

Only May Fontaine seemed unhappy. She smiled when Samantha told her the news, and she wished her happiness, but Samantha could see that it was forced. Samantha knew that May's sadness was not for Cecil. May knew Samantha's true feelings about Trevor Collins, and although she would not say anything about it directly, her eyes were full of sympathy as she embraced her.

"If you need anything," May said, "anything at all, Sammie, always feel free to come to me. I will help you all I can."

"Thank you, Mrs Fontaine," Samantha said, forcing herself to smile too. "I appreciate it."

Trevor wasted no time in preparing the house for Samantha's mother, and Samantha and her mother moved in not a single month after the engagement. At least one good thing had come from this arrangement, Samantha thought. Her mother's joy was beyond anything Samantha had seen in her since her father had died. The new home was airy, with plenty of windows to let in the light, and strong walls to keep things cosy and warm in winter. Trevor's family provided them with new furniture as well, and although Samantha insisted on continuing to run the fish stall until the wedding, her mother took a far more leisurely approach.

"I don't like you working," Trevor said to her warmly one day, as she sat down for dinner with him and his parents. "There's no need anymore."

"People rely on me and my mama," she said. "We must give them time to adjust to the change."

No one knew that Samantha was squirreling away a little of the income each day, only a small amount at first, so that her mother would not notice, but as her mama became less and less interested in the business, Samantha was able to stash more away. She hid it in a pouch under a loose floorboard beneath her bed, and never went near it while her mother was home. Even with all her hard work, she was unable to save much, but it was something, at least. She hoped for enough money to get transport to London, and to pay for a month or two of rent, while she searched for work. She might be able to find employment in a household, she thought, or a factory. As long as it took her far away from Bristol and Trevor Collins and his family.

She would not marry a brute such as him if she could at all escape it.

As the months passed, Samantha could not help feeling even more trapped. Trevor's father would not continue to house her mother if she ran. What would happen to her then? She would have no money, no place to live, and barely any business left at the stall. Trevor might even take his anger and disappointment out her mama. He seemed the vindictive sort, and if he could not find Samantha, she could not be certain he would not attack her mother in her place.

Every morning, as the sun rose, Samantha headed down to the beach and looked out across the water. She thought of Cecil, and she prayed to God for a miracle to save her. She could not leave without causing great harm to her mother, her only family. She could not stay without causing great harm to herself. She needed help.

She did not truly believe anyone was listening.

Her skin crawled whenever Trevor pulled her in to steal a kiss from her, and her arms were bruised from the punishing way he seized her and shifted her about. Summer faded, and then autumn, and the weather turned cold. Christmas was a far richer affair that year than the one before, with Samantha and her mother sharing the feast at the Collins. Trevor gave her a large, heavy necklace and fastened it around her neck, and Samantha shivered as she felt its weight against her heart.

On the morning of the day before her wedding, Samantha rose early and pulled her stash of money from its hiding place. She considered packing a bag as well, but she did not want her absence to be noticed. She still did not know what she intended to do. Could she really abandon her mother to her fate? Perhaps she should simply marry Trevor and make of this life what she could. Was her own freedom really worth the poverty that she and her mother would face, and the loneliness inherent in being forced to leave her entire life behind?

She wandered down to the docks and sat on the railing like she and Cecil often had as children, watching the sailors work and the ships come in. She must look terribly unladylike, she thought, but she found she did not care. Trevor would be furious, but that only made her more determined to do it.

She stared at out the water, and she prayed for a miracle, or a sign of what she ought to do.

She was about to turn away when she noticed a large ship on the horizon. It was a huge iron ocean liner, steam-powered, with pipes standing between the sails, although the steam engine did not seem to be working, and the pipes emitted no smoke. The ship was battered and worn, but it sailed resolutely forward, heading for the docks.

As it got closer, Samantha frowned. It looked so familiar to her. It must have been a replacement for the Santa

Lucia, built in the same design. She leaned forward, watching it. Was this the sign she had been asking for?

The ship looked as close to wrecked as Samantha thought it was possible to be while still sailing. Then she caught sight of the worn name on the hull, and she was so shocked that she almost fell from the railing.

It was the Santa Lucia.

CHAPTER FOURTEEN

I t couldn't be the Santa Lucia. She must be hallucinating. Samantha blinked, but the ship did not change.

She leapt from the railing and ran to the nearest sailor. "Do you see that?" she shouted. "Do you see that ship?" She pointed at the boat approaching the dock, and the sailor, looking irritated, looked up.

"Yeah, I see it, miss," he said. "My eyes work, just the same as yours." Then he did a doubletake and looked at the ship again. "It can't be," he said.

"You see it too?" Samantha said. "The Santa Lucia?"

The sailor raised up a shout, and soon everyone on the docks was crowding around the railing, staring at the ship coming in. The news spread through town too, and more and more people raced to the docks to watch it, the loved ones of the passengers and crew frantic with hope. Samantha could hardly dare imagine that Cecil might be alive on that ship. It seemed too much to wish for. But the ship drew nearer, and the name on its prow grew clearer and clearer.

"Sammie!" May Fontaine said. She ran up to the younger girl and grabbed her arm. "Sammie, is it true?"

Samantha could only nod and point at the ship. May staggered, her knees almost giving out underneath her, and Samantha caught her, holding her steady.

"Could it really be?" May murmured. "Oh, please let him be alive."

The two women embraced one another, their eyes fixed on the ship. It pulled into port, and the men leapt into activity to help those aboard it disembark.

The first person to climb from the Santa Lucia was a young man that Samantha recognised but could not name. He had been a member of the same crew as Cecil. A woman who must have been his mother let out a shriek from the crowd and ran toward him, pulling him into a sobbing embrace.

More people disembarked, ten, then twenty, and Samantha searched every face. She recognised many of them, but none of them were Cecil.

Her heart began to sink as the flow of people from the boat slowed. Whatever had happened to the Santa Lucia,

Cecil could not have survived. But then one last figure appeared on deck, and Samantha could not stop her cry of joy and relief.

It was Cecil. Not exactly as she remembered him, thinner, with longer hair and a beard about his chin, but Cecil none-the-less. Cecil looked across the dock at the noise, and when his eyes met Samantha, he broke into a huge grin. She ran forward, stumbling in her haste to reach him, and the crowd drew back to allow her to pass.

Cecil ran down the gangplank and swept her into his waiting arms. She sobbed against his chest, holding onto to him so tightly that he must have found it difficult to breathe, but he did not let go. He was solid and warm and definitely, definitely real. Not a ghost, not a hallucination, but him.

"I thought you were dead," she sobbed. "I thought that you'd died, I thought—"

"I know," Cecil said. "I know, I know. I'm sorry. I came back as soon as I could."

"Your mama," Samantha said. "She's here, she's alive, she—"

May Fontaine's shout of joy interrupted her, and Samantha pulled back to allow Cecil's mother to pull him into her arms. She rocked him back and forth, her hand pressed to the back of his head like he was still a small child, and Cecil wrapped his arms around his mother's back, tears streaming down his cheeks, and allowed himself to be held.

"Cecil," his mother said. "Cecil, my darling boy. You're alive. You're alive."

An hour later, and Cecil's entire family was gathered in the kitchen, listening to his tale.

"We were attacked by pirates," he said, "like you heard. Not everyone made it, but most of us did. The Santa Lucia was far too big and obvious to be of use to them as a boat, but they stripped it of everything they could, and left it in the cove as a sort of trophy, I suppose. We were with them for over a year, I reckon."

"You were a pirate?" Jane asked, sounding thrilled.

"Not willingly," Cecil said with a grimace. "But they weren't the worst sort. More interested in stealing loot than in hurting people. We just knew we had to keep our eyes and ears open, and our wits about us, or we'd never be able to go home."

"How did you escape?" Samantha asked breathlessly.

"Captain Rupert," Cecil said. "He said one day that he was going to get home to Bristol or die trying. We all started secretly preparing the Santa Lucia to leave. But they found us out, just before we could set sail. Captain Rupert

—he didn't make it." Cecil shook his head, tears in his eyes. "And the rest of us, we just sailed, as fast as we could. Which wasn't fast at all. It's been months and months since it happened, but the ship was so worn, and the engines and propellers barely worked. We had to travel using the wind most of the time, and the wind can't make a ship that big move very fast."

"Why didn't you stop and find another vessel?" his mother asked. "Why didn't you send a note?"

"We were scared," Cecil said, "of the pirates catching us or figuring out where we were going. Their ships were all faster than the Santa Lucia, so they could have intercepted us if they'd known where to look. We were lucky to get out of it alive. So we just kept sailing. Didn't say a word to anyone."

"Did you really think they would chase you?"

"We didn't know," Cecil said. "But we took a bunch of their supplies when we left. I wouldn't be surprised if they wanted them back. Plus, escaping wouldn't sit kindly with them, I'd reckon."

"Oh, Cecil, you're so brave," his mother said, throwing her arms around him.

They all talked for a while longer, and then Cecil glanced at Samantha. "Maybe you and I could take a walk," he said. "Talk alone?"

Samantha nodded, barely daring to speak for joy, and the two of them headed out onto the street, making their way towards the water.

"I'm sorry," Cecil said, "if I hurt you."

"It's worth it," Samantha said, "to see you alive again."

He smiled. Then he rubbed the back of his head, looking nervous. "I know I was gone a long time," he said. "I understand if you found someone else. A sweetheart, or a husband, or—"

"No," Samantha said. "I've never loved anyone but you."

Cecil broke into a relieved smile. "Truly?"

"Mama's been pushing me to marry Trevor Collins," she said, "but I never wanted to. But she threatened to kick me out, so I told her I would. We were due to get married tomorrow, but I never meant to do it. I was trying to work up the courage to run away when I saw your ship."

"So, you don't intend to marry him?" Cecil asked.

"Never!" Samantha cried. "I gave my heart away long ago."

"I know I can't offer you much," Cecil said. "But I have some money saved. Enough to rent a bigger place, and to buy a fishing boat. I've had more than enough adventures for a lifetime. I could sail out of Bristol, and never have to leave you for more than a few hours again. If you'll have me, of course."

"Of course, I will have you," Samantha said. "I already promised you, didn't I? We said we would be married the very next time you returned home to Bristol. We didn't quite manage to complete the ceremony on the docks, like we said, but we can make some allowances for circumstances, I suppose, and wait a day. But no longer than that. I don't ever intend to let you go again, Cecil Fontaine."

CHAPTER FIFTEEN

Cecil and Samantha married the very next day. Instead of being wed to a man she feared, Samantha was reunited with her love again, and she was so happy she felt she must be floating.

Samantha's mother was less pleased with developments. She ranted to Samantha about her foolishness, but Samantha would not be dissuaded. She fulfilled her duty to her mother by giving her the money she had saved over the year, enough for a couple of months' rent at least, and told her that she would always be happy to see her, as long as she accepted Cecil for who he was.

Trevor Collins was predictably furious, and he and his family muttered about that harlot from the docks to anyone who would listen, but they found that Bristol society was very much against them. The newspapers loved the story of the lost ship miraculously returned, and the wedding between Cecil and Samantha the very next day was the sort of love story that gossips dreamed of. Everyone in Bristol knew about the seemingly doomed lovers' joyful reunion, and their generosity allowed Cecil and Samantha to make their wedding a beautiful one, despite the lack of Trevor's wealth.

Samantha, refusing to keep anything from Trevor, returned her original wedding dress and got married in her Sunday best, with flowers woven in her hair in tribute to how the pair of them had met.

The couple soon moved into their own home, and Cecil purchased a small fishing boat with which they could make their living. Samantha continued to run the fish stall, and the legend of their reunion and the quality of Samantha's cooking together made it one of the most popular places to get lunch in all of town. Once Samantha's mother saw that Cecil was able to provide for her daughter, and had no intention of sailing out of Bristol again, she came around to support the marriage, and Samantha forgave her for all that had happened before, knowing that her mother had truly only had their future wellbeing at heart.

Finally, Samantha was officially part of the Fontaine family, as she had been in her heart for most of her life, and she delighted to spend time with her new sisters and mother and uncle. The family spent many fond evenings together, and every time Samantha looked at her husband, she remembered how close she had come to losing him, and how grateful she was to be beside him again.

Samantha and Cecil were never parted again, and they grew old in happiness together, with their family, their children, and later their grandchildren around them. Their grandchildren never seemed to fully believe the legend of Cecil's disappearance and return, but by that time, Cecil had embellished the story so fully that even he was unsure what the truth was any more. All anyone knew for certain was that the world had smiled on the Fontaine family, and they knew the value of love and faith, and felt it in their hearts every day for the rest of their lives.

THANK YOU FOR CHOOSING A PUREREAD BOOK!

We hope you enjoyed the story, and as a way to thank you for choosing PureRead we'd like to send you this free book, and other fun reader rewards...

Click here for your free copy of Whitechapel Waif
PureRead.com/victorian

Thanks again for reading.
See you soon!

HAVE YOU READ?

THE MILL DAUGHTER'S COURAGE

Now that you have read 'Poor Miss Cole And The Cobbler's Boy' why not lose yourself in another heartwarming Victorian Romance?

Doubtless, your heart has been touched by the story of Poor Miss Cole and her long road to happiness.

Heart-touching tales continue in another PureRead family saga called *The Mill Daughter's Courage* - the story of an English mill girl, Daisy Barlow.

Daisy's story begins amidst the shadows and perils of a foreboding industrial mill. Here amidst the gloom, Daisy Barlow discovers pockets of happiness in her mother, Vera, and her twin sister, Janet – until tragedy strikes...

The untimely death of her beloved sister and the soul-crushing grief of her mother push Daisy to an agonising juncture – one that leaves her all alone to **fend for herself against seemingly insurmountable odds**. But Daisy is not a quitter!

Far from defeated, her spirit remains unyielding, fuelled by the unwavering belief in her mother's eventual recovery and the promise of a brighter future. Surely her sister's death was not in vain.

Will sweet Daisy survive this cruel world to find her Happily Ever After?

For your enjoyment here are the first chapters of her story...

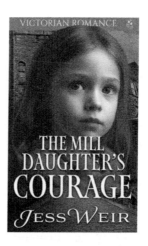

Daisy Barlow sneezed so loudly that it could almost be heard over the dreadful din of the machinery. Having spent half her young life working in the mill, it was a wonder that Daisy's nose was still so sensitive to the tiny flying particles of cotton lint.

Janet, who was under one of the machines hastily tying the two ends of a snapped thread, slid out and stood upright, grinning like a fool and mimicking the motion of a sneeze before pretending to cover her ears against the sound.

Daisy laughed and shook her head. Her twin sister always made her laugh. However bad the day was, Janet Barlow could see some good in it, or if not the good, then at least a little humour. Daisy didn't know how other children managed the long days at the mill without a twin of their own to take the edge off things.

Daisy's attention quickly returned to her work. Her mother, Vera, had seen her beloved girls out of the corner of her eye and quickly shook her head from side to side. Daisy knew her mother was just worried that Mr Baker would see and reprimand the girls or, worse still, dock their already meagre wages. And, of course, there was the ever-present threat of being reported to Mr Wainwright for misbehaving. He was famous for his short temper and penchant for the arbitrary dismissal of a mill worker without so much as a minute's hearing.

Turning to look at her mother, Daisy gave her a tiny nod to put her mind at rest and turned her eyes back to the loom. In return, Vera smiled at her daughter, so briefly that nobody could have accused her of not getting on with her work. Over the years, the family of three had developed their own system of silent communication in a world which was anything but.

Daisy turned her attention back to the shuttle quill she was loading with thread. She needed to be fast for Mr Baker didn't like the little things taking too much time. *Time was money*, that's what Mr Baker always said. Of course, for Daisy and her mother and sister, *time* was a *pittance*, for their pay barely kept them alive.

Daisy could see that Janet had already moved on from her amusement and was fully absorbed in wiping down. As far as Daisy could tell, it was just about the worst job in the entire mill. The worker, usually the younger children, would have to dart between the two heaviest parts of the power loom to wipe it down. In its practice, it wasn't any better or worse than many other jobs in the mill. To Daisy, however, the noise was horrendous. It was nothing compared to the inattentiveness of the man holding the carriage of the loom back on its brakes. Add in the sheer weight of the loom carriages —it made the whole thing more life-threatening.

Although she gave every appearance of working on her own task, Daisy watched the wiping down like a hawk when Janet was the child sent in to do it. She wanted to be ready to pull on the brakes herself if the man in charge of them let them go too quickly.

The problem was that Janet was small. They were both thirteen years old, but Daisy was tall, and Janet was short and slight, like a tiny fairy. She was still able to take the same awful tasks that were reserved for children. At thirteen, Daisy and Janet were hardly that. No, children were five, six or at the most seven. At thirteen, childhood was long gone, if it had ever truly been there in the first place.

As she wound the thread back onto the shuttle, Daisy felt every nerve ending standing to attention. She moved a little to her right, closer to David Langley, the man standing at the brake lever. With her eyes darting back and forth between her sister and David, Daisy felt the dreadful sense of anxiety which seemed to sweep over her so many times in her working day. It was so common that it had come to feel like a perpetual state.

It was nearing the end of the day. A day which had begun sixteen hours before. It was the time of day, often referred to by the little ones as *the death time*. It was a disturbingly accurate description, for the last two hours of the working day were the hours in which most of the accidents happened. People who had worked for so many hours were exhausted enough, without the ceaseless noise of the machinery making it even harder to concentrate.

Shuttles banged from side to side, the engines roared, and the very walls of the mill seemed almost to shake. There was no escape from the din, and it was debilitating. All in all, *the death time* should have come as no surprise to anybody. Who could possibly concentrate as well in the *death time* as they had first thing in the morning after a little rest and a little quiet?

When Janet slid out from beneath the mule of the machine, Daisy breathed a sigh of relief. David let go of the brakes immediately, as he always did. Janet was barely clear of the loom when the carriage slid back with a bang loud enough to compete with so many other dreadful sounds. Langley always let go of the brakes like that. It was ingrained into them all that the machines should not be idle for long. When the machines stopped, the pay stopped. David Langley was in no better position than the Barlow family, and she could understand a poor man's desire to get the machine going straight away. Perhaps, he might have been a little less hasty had the person doing the wiping down been his own daughter or sister.

With her nerves shredded, Daisy knew that the final hour of the working day couldn't pass by fast enough. She needed to be out of the noise and out of danger, letting go of the fear for a few hours until morning rolled around once more.

Janet was chattering to her as the girls and their mother got ready for the short journey home. It was a relief to get a little cool air, having suffered the tremendous heat of the mill for so many hours.

"I thought today would never end!" Janet said brightly, shouting instead of speaking, as so many mill workers did as they readjusted to the world outside of the unspeakable noise.

"Me too. I've almost sneezed my brains clean out today." Daisy was always ready to join in a little banter and have her beloved twin raise her spirits on the way home.

"Almost?" Janet was still loud, still adjusting. "They came right out, I saw them. They flew out of your nose and landed in Mr Baker's deep pockets!"

"Janet!" their mother hissed, looking over her shoulder.

"He's not here, is he, Mama? He's not out here with those of us of the bare-foot brigade searching for the right clogs to walk home in." Janet was giggling.

"Maybe he isn't here, my love, but there are them as would run to him and tell him if they thought it would do them some benefit. And think of Mr Wainwright! He's as like to throw out an entire family as throw out just one noisy girl, isn't he? Then where shall we be?" She sobered her voice. "And what would God think of us? Talking about another rudely behind their backs. It isn't the Christian or the kind thing to do, no matter how mean Mr Wainwright may get,"

"Sorry, Mama," Janet was quiet now, her pretty face full of heartfelt apology as she eased her bare feet into her clogs.

Daisy smiled, Janet was the light of her life, but she knew their mother was right. They must always be careful when they spoke. Even at the end of the day when a myriad of workers, all of whom had worked barefoot in the mill room to avoid sparks from their clog irons igniting the snow-like cotton dust which covered the floors, were re-shooing themselves for the walk home.

Daisy wrapped her shawl around herself tightly, making her way to the open door of the mill and out into the cool evening air. Working in the almost crippling heat and stifled recirculated air of the mill was almost like working in another country. The outside air always felt like something of a shock at the end of the working day, even if it was a blessed relief to draw a breath which didn't fill the lungs with soft cotton dust.

"What shall we have for our tea tonight?" Janet asked, chattering happily as they walked home, their clogs tapping a rhythmic beat as they went. "Shall we have venison?" she went on, laughing and completely recovered from their mother's telling-off.

"Or shall we have salmon and trout?" Daisy played along, always feeling a burst of relief at this time every day that the three of them had made it out of the mill for another day alive and with their full complement of fingers.

"Or shall we keep a hold of the real world and just eat the potato and cabbage stew we've been heating and re-heating all week long?" Vera stated with a sigh. She did, however, look at her girls and smile.

"Aye, let's do that! You can't beat cabbage at the end of a long day." Janet was as high-spirited at night as she was first thing in the morning.

"You've a fair humour on you, child, I'll give you that, but you tire me right enough," Vera said and laughed.

"Just think, in three days it will be Sunday. Nothing to do but go to church. No sounds but the birdsong to replace the looms." Daisy was getting in the spirit of things.

"Not you too, Daisy!" Vera said and chuckled. "Not my sensible child! We've cleaning to be doing on Sunday as you very well know. That shameless landlord will be poking his beak into things, looking for some excuse to put the rent up again. No, my girl, we'll need to have the floor scrubbed and the mattresses tidied away in their corners. As the saying goes, there's no rest for the wicked."

"Then we must truly be the most wicked three females on earth, Mama, for there really is never a moment of rest," Daisy said and began to feel deflated.

"That won't help, my little chick. Try to stay above it all like your sister does. It won't do to dwell."

It won't do to dwell was a phrase their mother had used day in, day out since their father had left them six years before when the twins were just seven. Vera had been right, of course, it really didn't do to dwell. There wasn't time to dwell, not even for the tiny girls who had been forced to work in the mill alongside their mother just to make ends meet.

Perhaps if their father had stayed, Janet wouldn't have to crawl between the loom carriage and the roller beam every day. Perhaps Daisy wouldn't have to swallow down the ball of fear in her throat each time. But Tom Barlow had gone, and he wasn't coming back. He'd left Burnley with his lover and had moved to goodness-knew-where to live in sin with her. Perhaps they had moved far enough away that they might pretend to be man and wife. Either way, Daisy Barlow would never, ever forgive him. Mother taught forgiveness, and how everyone deserved it, "just as Jesus forgave us all" she would say – but Daisy didn't think a father who abandoned his family deserved forgiveness at all.

"Don't you think it's funny that Mr Baker is called Mr Baker, but he's not a baker, he works in a mill?" Janet said, breaking Daisy out of her dark train of thought. "And that Mr Wainwright is called Mr Wainwright, but he isn't a wainwright, but the man who owns the mill. I suppose a relation of his must have been a wainwright at some time, don't you think, Mama?"

"I think you need to do less thinking, lass, if that's the best you can come up with!" Vera said, and they all laughed. "Come on, girls, let's get home!"

Janet stopped suddenly, and stood upright as if in shock. "I think we shall have the salmon and trout on Tuesday in three weeks! For that is a special day!"

Daisy giggled, understanding her sister's joke.

Vera smiled. "And why is that day so special?"

Daisy's eyes seemed to twinkle even brighter than usual. "Because that Tuesday is our birthday!"

"Have you not swept that lot up yet, Janet?" Vera Barlow asked with mild exasperation.

"Mama, I swept it up twice already. I don't know where it all comes from. That ceiling has been peeling for so long now that it's a wonder we're not just looking up at the clear sky!"

"Come on, Janet, let me sweep for a while," Daisy said and smiled at her sister as she took the broom. "She's right though, Mama, I remember this ceiling being in a dreadful state when we first came here after Father... well... when we first came here."

"Six years of peeling, day in, day out. It must be a miracle of some kind that it hasn't peeled itself completely away." Janet sat on an upturned bucket in the middle of the room, the bucket she was to fill with water from the pump outside to wash the bare wooden floorboards of their one-room home in the Burnley slums.

"It'd be a bigger miracle if Joe Hamill had the place painted just once. And the wooden window frames are so rotten that as much cold air flies through this room when the windows are closed as when they are open. He really *is* a shameless charlatan, Mama," Daisy said, already having half the room swept.

"Be that as it may, there isn't a right lot we can do about it, Daisy. I don't know what sort of places you think the three of us can afford on our money." Sometimes Vera was just down, struggling beneath the weight of so much responsibility and hopelessness. "This is as good as our sort get."

"Mama, I know you don't mean that. It might be all we get, but it's not what we deserve. Joe Hamill might have clawed his way to own a rundown building or two, but he soon forgot where he came from, didn't he? He soon learned, like them rich ones do, that the best way of making money is either out of our pockets or off our backs. If the ceiling is peeling away to nothing, Mama, it's Joe Hamill's shame, not ours." Still sweeping, Daisy turned to look over her shoulder and smile at her mother. "The three of us do everything we can in this life, don't we?"

"That we do, my little chick. That we do," Vera said and smiled back, making Daisy feel relieved.

By the time the Barlow family had paid their rent every week, there was very little left for anything else. The slums were the cheapest possible rent, but that rent was still far too high for what they received. It was a trap that the working poor fell into. A trap set by those who knew their circumstances well and had already discovered the best ways to profit by those circumstances. To keep a roof over their head, a poor family had nowhere else to go but the slums. That being the case, the landlord was free to allow the housing to fall into any state of disrepair he chose. Always reminding his tenants that if they were not happy, they might leave at any time. Always knowing that they couldn't afford to be anywhere better.

Daisy wasn't a vengeful girl, but she certainly spent a good part of her day hoping that the people who had done the worst in this life, taken advantage of others, made money from their plight, would suffer for it one day as she and her kind had suffered. And it *was* suffering to live in such a place, especially for a girl who could remember what life was like before her father had disappeared.

They'd never been wealthy, far from it, but they'd rented a tiny two up two down terraced house in a slightly cleaner part of Burnley. Knowing how to read and write, Tom Barlow had occasionally found himself in jobs which paid a little better than the rest. It certainly wasn't enough for luxuries, but at least his wife and daughters had a little more by way of clothing than one dress for the week and one for Sundays. When he had still been at home, they'd all had a bonnet. However, years of wear and growing had seen them all bonnet-less for some time now.

Their room was on the ground floor of a two-story brick-built house. The walls had creeping mould where the damp from the outside made its way through the gaps and rotten woodwork after years of neglect. Even though it never seemed to go anywhere, Daisy spent a good part of every Sunday with a brush and a pail of hot water trying to get rid of it.

There was a fireplace in the room, over which the family cooked their meagre meals. There was a rail affixed to the chimney breast which held the family's only two pans and one spoon for stirring. There was an iron rail, which ended in a flat plate, set inside the fireplace, somewhere to set down a pan for cooking.

Their beds were no better than narrow mattresses on the floor, mattresses they'd had so long that Daisy couldn't even remember how and where they had acquired them, she only knew that they had never been brand-new to the family. No doubt countless people had slept on them before they'd made their way into the Barlow family's small abode.

They left the mattresses on the floor all week long, made up ready for them to crawl into after a long day's work. However, on Sundays, the mattresses were heaved up on their end, leaned against a wall, and covered with a sheet. Sunday was a day when Joe Hamill might appear at any moment, and Vera not only wanted to avoid him declaring the place to be a mess and adding a shilling to the rent, but she had her own pride too. Their home might not have been much, but she was determined to keep it clean and decent.

In fact, Vera was so determined that there was only a pot to be used in emergencies. Otherwise, she and her daughters wandered out of the back of the house, day or night, to the shared privy at the far end of the row. Daisy hated the shared privy. Nobody ever seemed to take responsibility for keeping it clean, and as a result, it was an awful place.

"Have you not swept that lot up yet, Daisy?" Janet asked, parroting her mother's earlier words and grinning like a court jester.

"I never knew anybody as cheeky as you!" Daisy said, trying to sound stern but unable to keep her amusement out of her voice, much less her face.

"What would life be like if I wasn't around to be cheeky anymore? Dull, that's what!" Janet said and got to her feet, picking up the bucket she'd been sitting on and heading out of the door to fill it at the pump.

As Daisy swept up the last curls of peeled paint, she looked over at her mother. They smiled at one another; they knew that life was made better by Janet and her cheeky ways.

It was late on Wednesday, and Daisy could hardly believe that they still had three full sixteen-hour days of work to do before Sunday came around again. Why was it that Sunday passed by so quickly and the rest of the week dragged along in noise and dust and worry?

"Daisy," Mr Baker had come up beside her and bellowed in her ear, trying to make himself heard over the machinery. "Go across to the back loom, the thread keeps snapping. I know your hands aren't tiny, but you're nimble enough. But mind you concentrate; I don't want to have to shut off the machine if you lose a finger in there."

Daisy stared at him for a moment before a gentle shove propelled her in the right direction. She didn't want to be on the other side of the mill, she always liked to have her mother and sister close enough to see. However, Mr Baker, the man who managed the day-to-day running of the mill for Mr Wainwright, was not a man to be argued with. So, Daisy hurried through the room, her bare feet kicking up the soft, fluffy cotton dust as she went.

The other loom really did need looking at and looking at properly. The thread was snapping every few minutes, and there was clearly either a problem with the bobbins or the gap settings on the loom itself. Either way, if she simply kept re-tying the threads, somebody would later be complaining about having to trim the loose ones off the fabric, possibly even Mr Baker himself.

After almost half an hour of tying the threads, the decision was made to shut down the loom and fix the problem. Daisy could see the disappointment on so many faces, none of them keen to take the drop in pay that inevitably resulted from one of the looms going down, whether it was their fault or not.

It was time for Daisy to get out of the way and Mr Baker, without words, pointed her back across to her original work of making sure that the shuttles flew through the threads easily on each pass. Her mother was doing the same job a few feet away from her, her focus fully absorbed. As Daisy resumed her own work, she scanned the room for any sign of Janet.

Not seeing her anywhere, she felt that little sense of panic she always felt. This time, however, there was a sudden prickling at the back of her neck, a sense of dreadful foreboding. Taking her eyes off her own work entirely, Daisy realised that one of the looms had been opened, its carriage drawn out and held back on brakes. No doubt Janet, small and nimble, was inside, crouched down, wiping away the dust which choked the looms so regularly.

As always, Daisy fixed her attention on David Langley. She could see that the man regularly looked over his shoulder at the unfolding drama of the dormant loom at the back of the room. With his hand on the brake lever, Daisy held her breath. Why couldn't the man just concentrate on what he was doing, instead of worrying what the closed loom was going to do to his pay packet?

With the greatest sense that something was about to go wrong, Daisy felt a horrible feeling in the pit of her stomach. Even though nothing had yet happened, she had a sense that it was already too late. Daisy left her post and began to cross to where David was. She crouched down as she made her way, looking for any sign of Janet and seeing her similarly crouched just exactly where she expected to see her; between the carriage and the roller beam.

As if it was always going to happen, the distracted David Langley, likely as bone-tired as the rest of them and in need of a break, absentmindedly pushed at the brake lever. Daisy opened her mouth to scream, her arms spread wide as she tried to get the man's attention. However, her scream died in the noise of the room, and she knew that it was already too late the moment he had pushed the brake lever.

The carriage flew back instantly, that horrible bang as it settled into place once more. Daisy dropped to the floor, scrabbling on her hands and knees, trying to find her sister. Perhaps the only saving grace, when she did find her, was to know that it would have been quick. Janet wouldn't have lingered.

Crushed between the back of the loom carriage and the immovable roller beam, Janet Barlow's head lolled to one side, her chest and shoulders flattened. The heavy machinery pinned her there in such a position, such a garish, awful position, that Daisy knew she would never forget it for the rest of her life.

Daisy, on her hands and knees, was violently sick. Bit by bit, the room began to fall silent. There was a commotion behind her, all around her the men were powering down the looms. Bare feet were running backwards and forwards in a blind panic. It was the first time in the six years that Daisy had worked in the mill that the machines had all been powered down at once, and it seemed that the sudden silence caused a great pressure inside her ears, inside her head.

Suddenly realising that there was somebody at her side, Daisy tried to turn to look, but couldn't take her eyes off her sister. Her beloved twin sister; the other half of her. The funny half, the light-hearted half, the tiny and most precious half.

It was only when she heard her mother's heartbroken screams that she realised that it was *she* crouched down by her side, *she* who was staring across at the broken, lifeless body of the daughter she couldn't reach...

How will Daisy survive without her beloved twin sister to cheer her days? Will her mother's grief consume all that is good and pure leaving nothing but devastation?

Discover all in the compelling new book by Jess Weir, The Mill Daughters Courage.

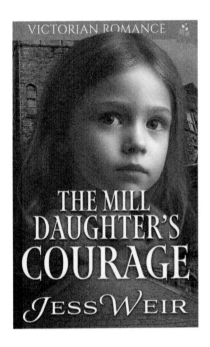

Start Reading Now

LOVE VICTORIAN ROMANCE?

If you enjoyed this story why not continue straight away with other books in our PureRead Victorian Romance library?

Read them all...

Orphan Christmas Miracle

An Orphan's Escape

The Lowly Maiden's Loyalty

Ruby of the Slums

The Dancing Orphan's Second Chance

Cotton Girl Orphan & The Stolen Man

Victorian Slum Girl's Dream

The Lost Orphan of Cheapside

Dora's Workhouse Child

Saltwick River Orphan

Workhouse Girl and The Veiled Lady

OUR GIFT TO YOU

AS A WAY TO SAY THANK YOU WE WOULD LOVE TO SEND YOU THIS BEAUTIFUL STORY FREE OF CHARGE.

Our Reader List is 100% FREE

Click here for your free copy of Whitechapel Waif

PureRead.com/victorian

At PureRead we publish books you can trust. Great tales without smut or swearing, but with all of the mystery and romance you expect from a great story.

Be the first to know when we release new books, take part in our fun competitions, and get surprise free books in your inbox by signing up to our Reader list.

As a thank you you'll receive an exclusive copy of Whitechapel Waif - a beautiful book available only to our subscribers...

Click here for your free copy of Whitechapel Waif

PureRead.com/victorian

Printed in Great Britain
by Amazon

37857478R00088